Oh! My
Useless
Goddess!

KONOSUBA:
GOD'S BLESSING ON THIS
WONDERFUL WORLD 1!

Darkness

"Ah, the cabbages were so lively this year!"

"I wanna go back to Japan..."

Kazuma

"Behold my power!"

KONOSUBA: GOD'S BLESSING ON THIS WONDERFUL WORLD

Oh! My Useless Goddess!

CONTENTS

KONOSUBA: GOD'S BLESSING ON THIS WONDERFUL WORLD!

Oh! My Useless Goddess!

1

NATSUME AKATSUKI

ILLUSTRATION BY
KURONE MISHIMA

YEN ON

NEW YORK

KONOSUBA: GOD'S BLESSING ON THIS WONDERFUL WORLD! 1

NATSUME AKATSUKI

Translation by Kevin Steinbach
Cover art by Kurone Mishima

KONO SUBARASHII SEKAI NI SHUKUFUKU WO! Volume 1 AA, DAMEGAMI SAMA
©2013 Natsume Akatsuki, Kurone Mishima
First published in Japan in 2013 by KADOKAWA CORPORATION, Tokyo.
English translation rights arranged with KADOKAWA CORPORATION, Tokyo through TUTTLE-MORI AGENCY, INC., Tokyo.

English translation © 2017 by Yen Press, LLC

Yen On
1290 Avenue of the Americas
New York, NY 10104

Visit us at yenpress.com
facebook.com/yenpress
twitter.com/yenpress
yenpress.tumblr.com
instagram.com/yenpress

First Yen On Edition: February 2017

Yen On is an imprint of Yen Press, LLC.
The Yen On name and logo are trademarks of Yen Press, LLC.

Library of Congress Cataloging-in-Publication Data
Names: Akatsuki, Natsume, author. | Mishima, Kurone, 1991– illustrator. | Steinbach, Kevin, translator.
Title: Konosuba, God's blessing on this wonderful world! / Natsume Akatsuki ; illustration by Kurone Mishima ; translation by Kevin Steinbach.
Other titles: Kono subarashi sekai ni shukufuku o. English
Description: First Yen On edition. | New York, NY : Yen On, 2017– Contents: v. 1. Oh! my useless goddess!
Identifiers: LCCN 2016052009| ISBN 9780316553377 (v. 1 : paperback)
Subjects: | CYAC: Fantasy. | Future life—Fiction. | Adventure and adventurers—Fiction. | BISAC: FICTION / Fantasy / General.
Classification: LCC PZ7.1.A38 Ko 2017 | DDC [Fic]—dc23
LC record available at https://lccn.loc.gov/2016052009

ISBNs: 978-0-316-55337-7 (paperback)
978-0-316-46872-5 (ebook)

10 9

LSC-C

Printed in the United States of America

Character

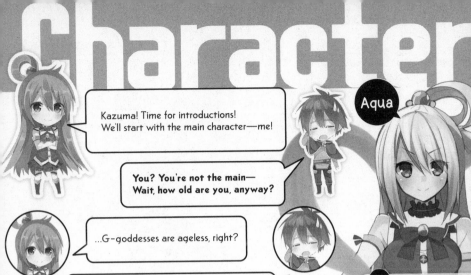

Aqua

Kazuma! Time for introductions! We'll start with the main character—me!

You? You're not the main— Wait, how old are you, anyway?

...G-goddesses are ageless, right?

Why'd you hesitate? Are you pulling my leg?

Questions, questions. You're just some hikiNEET. Who *do* you think I am?

The goddess of party tricks?

Age **Unknown**

Job **Arch-priest**

A goddess who gives guidance to the young and deceased. In the parallel world she's sent to with Kazuma, she is worshipped by the Axis Church as "the goddess Aqua"...not that anyone there believes she's actually a deity.

Megumin

Hmph! Now it is my turn! My name is Megumin! First among the spell-casters of the Crimson Magic Clan, and—

So, what's your real name?

My real name?

...

If you have a problem with my name, let us hear it!

...I guess we have to do Darkness next.

Hey, do not ignore me!

13 Age Job

Arch-wizard

An exceptionally talented magic-user even among the Crimson Magic Clan. Obsessed with the überpowerful spell Explosion, she is neither capable of nor interested in using any other magic. Favorite thing: Explosion. Special skill: Explosion. Hobby: Go ahead. Guess. (It's Explosion.)

Profiles

 What's wrong, Kazuma? Your clothes are a mess!

 Yeah—*someone* dropped a magical explosion on me. ✕

 Y-you got magically exploded? I'm so jealous...

Did you just say "jealous"?

 ...No.

Yes, you did. Why's your face red?

 Um, it's certainly not because I'm holding back trembles of excitement at the thought of being exploded in public.

Darkness

Age **18**

Job **Crusader**

A female Knight who specializes in defense. She looks tough, but in reality she's got a wild imagination and a serious masochistic streak. She likes being attacked by monsters, enjoying it as a sort of erotic play.

Kazuma Satou

16 Age

Job

Adventurer

A high school shut-in who loves anime, manga, and video games. He died in a traffic accident on the one day he left the house and wound up in a parallel world, along with Aqua.

Do I have to introduce *myself*?

Better let me handle it. All right! To wrap things up, allow me to introduce my minion!

Who's the minion?! And how come the main character's last, anyway?

...Minion.

No, no! Kazuma is my slave!

S-slave..?

 My party can't be this dysfunctional.

Prologue

"Kazuma Satou… Welcome to the Great Beyond. I'm sorry to tell you that you've passed on. It was a short life, but it's over now."

Those were the first words I heard upon finding myself in that bright white room.

It was so sudden, I had no idea what was going on. There was a little desk and a chair, like you'd find in an office. And sitting in the chair was the person notifying me of the end of my life.

If there are such things as goddesses, the woman in front of me certainly qualified.

She was more than just "cute" like the pop stars on TV—no human could match her beauty.

She had long hair the translucent blue of the sea on a clear day. It gave her a soft, gentle aura.

She looked to be about my age.

Her light-purple clothes fit perfectly, not too revealing but not hiding anything. She was wearing what we would call a "feather mantle," divine raiment like the ones in Japan's old stories.

This beauty stared at me with eyes the same light blue as her hair, blinking at my inability to understand what had happened.

I thought back on the last thing I could remember…

※

…Normally I stay locked in my room. Don't even go to school. But today, for once, I left the house. I wanted to get the limited Day One edition of a popular MMO that was coming out today, so I was up earlier than usual to claim my spot in line.

Yeah, I'm what people like to dismiss as a "*hikikomori*," someone so intensely introverted, they've withdrawn from society, living a life of isolation and never leaving their room. Others call me an "MMO junkie." Whatever. I secured my game and was heading home to try it out, spirits high. Then it happened.

A girl was walking ahead of me, playing with her phone. Judging by her uniform, she was enrolled at the same school as me.

The traffic light turned green, and she stepped into the crosswalk without even glancing left or right.

I saw the shadow loom over her.

It had to be a truck, bearing down on her at high speed.

I shoved her out of the way before I could think.

And then…

With a calm that surprised even me, I said quietly to the beautiful woman before me:

"…Can I just ask one thing?"

She nodded. "Of course."

"…That girl…the one I pushed out of the way. Is she alive?"

That was important to me. It was the first—and last—cool thing I'd done in my life. If it turned out I'd been too late, that I hadn't saved her—that would be awful.

"Sure. She's got a pretty bad broken leg, though."

Thank goodness…

That meant my death wasn't in vain. I was able to do something worthwhile with my life, even if only at the very end...

The beautiful girl cocked her head questioningly at my look of relief.

"Although, if you hadn't pushed her, she wouldn't have been hurt at all."

"......Huh?"

What did she just say?!

"That tractor would've stopped before hitting her. Obviously. It's a tractor. It doesn't even go that fast. Your dumb heroics were totally uncalled for. Pffft...hee-hee-hee!"

She sure knew how to make a good first impression. Not.

I guess it would be rude to smack her. But I really want to.

Never mind that. There was something more important to ask.

"What did you say? A *tractor*? Not a truck?"

"Yes, that's right. A tractor. You think that girl wouldn't have noticed if some huge truck was coming right at her? She would've gotten out of the way."

...Huh?

"Wait, so...I died getting run over by a tractor?"

"No, you died of shock. You were convinced a truck had hit you, and your body failed. I've been doing this a long time, but you're the first person I've met who died in such a weird way."

I was at a loss for words.

"Incidentally, you soiled yourself when you thought you were going to be hit by that tractor. They took you to the nearest hospital, and all the doctors and nurses were like, 'Whaaat? What a loser! (LOL),' and you died of a heart attack without even waking u—"

I threw my hands over my ears. "Stop iiiit! Please noooo, I don't wanna hear it! I don't need to hear how pathetic it was!"

She drew close to me and, with a smirk, whispered in my ear: "Your family got to the hospital just this minute, and before they could even grieve, they heard the cause of death and burst out laughi—"

"Stop! Stop! You're making this up, right? No one's ever died in such a pathetic way!"

She stood above me and giggled as I knelt on the ground, my head in my hands.

"All right. I guess I've let off enough steam for today. Nice to meet you, Kazuma Satou. My name is Aqua. I'm a goddess who gives guidance to those in Japan who die young. Now, then. Regardless of how amusing the circumstances of your demise may be, you have two choices."

This damn woman...!

All right, forget it. I had to let it go, or we'd never get anywhere.

"Option one: be reborn as a human, starting a completely new life. And option two: live like an old geezer in a heavenly place."

Talk about lose-lose.

"Hang on... What do you mean, 'heavenly place'? And what is 'living like an old geezer,' anyway?"

"Honestly, Heaven isn't as great a place as you humans imagine. The dead don't need to eat, and nothing is ever produced in the afterlife—so even if you wanted to cook something, there'd be no ingredients. Sorry to disappoint you, but Heaven's actually a real drag. No TV, no manga, no video games. Just a bunch of dead people. And since you're dead, you can't even hook up with anyone! I mean, you don't really have a body, right? It's just you and a bunch of spirits sitting around sunning yourselves and making small talk for all eternity."

What? No paradise? No video games? That's not Heaven. That's Hell.

I could start over as a baby...

Hang on—are those seriously my only choices?

I was clearly dejected, but the goddess gave me a huge smile.

"You're right. Who wants to go to a boring place like Heaven? And being reborn isn't so hot, either. You lose all your memories, and isn't that basically the same as saying *you*, Kazuma Satou, would cease to exist? Well! Have I got an offer for you…"

I smelled something fishy.

She saw I was wary, but Aqua only grinned even wider.

"You like video games, right?"

And then she proudly laid out her great proposal or whatever.

The long and short of it was this:

There's another world, different from our own, that is home to someone called the Demon King.

The Demon King's invading army threatens that world. It's a place of magic and monsters—in other words, a fantasy setting pretty much like those found in popular games like *Dragon Hunter* or *MonsterQuest*.

"So people who die in that world… Well, see, the majority of them were killed by the Demon King, right? And they don't want to go through that again. So most of them refuse to be reborn. That means fewer and fewer babies are getting born there, and eventually the world will be ruined! So we thought…why not send someone who died in some other world off to this threatened one?"

I can't imagine the headaches around that *immigration policy.*

"And we figured as long as we're sending someone, it might as well be someone who died young, a blank slate. We'd send them with their body and memory intact. What's more, since it would be silly to send someone over there just to die *again*, we decided to allow them to bring along any one thing they want. A powerful special ability, an incredible talent… Some people choose a legendary weapon… So how about it? You get another shot at life in a new world, and they get someone battle-ready to come to their aid. What do you think? Not bad, right?"

It really *wasn't* bad.

I could feel my excitement ramping up, though. I liked games, sure, but I never thought I'd have the chance to live in a world just like one.

But before that, first things first…

"Um, just asking, but—what about the language in this new world? Can I speak it?"

"No worries there. Through the kind support of us deities, the language will be loaded into your brain when you go over, allowing you to learn it instantaneously. You'll be able to read it, too, of course. There's a slim chance that it would result in an overload that makes you go *poof*, if you're not lucky. So! All that's left is to pick your awesome ability or gear."

"Wait, wait, wait, wait, wait. Did you just say I might go *poof*?"

"No, I didn't."

"Yeah, you did."

Even though she was a goddess, I found myself speaking bluntly, without any of the anxiety I'd felt until a few minutes ago.

…I had to admit, it was an attractive proposition.

True, I was worried I might go *poof*, but (not to brag) my luck had always been my only strong point, so I figured I would be fine.

Aqua thrust something like a catalog in front of my face.

"Take your pick. Any one thing. I'll give you power second to none. Look. This one's an amazing special ability. Here's a legendary sword. Come on, anything at all. Just say the word, and you can bring it with you to your new home."

I took the catalog from her and thumbed through the pages. It listed everything by name: "Super Strength," "Profound Magic," "the Sacred Sword Arondight," "Muramasa, the Demon Blade."

I got it. They wanted me to pick some power or item from this catalog.

Aww, man…how could I ever choose?

Maybe it was my gamer's intuition speaking, but everything seemed totally broken.

What to pick, what to pick? Well, if there was gonna be magic there, then of course I would have to try it! So maybe some power that would involve the use of magic…

"C'mon, hurry up, will you? It doesn't matter what you pick, anyway. No one's expecting anything from some *hikikomori* video game *otaku*, so just grab something and get outta here! Come on—we haven't got all eternity!"

"I-I'm not an *otaku*. And I died outdoors, so I'm not a *hikikomori*, either." My reply was quiet, and my voice trembled. Aqua, toying with her hair, answered with complete disinterest:

"Look, I don't care. You think you're the only dead guy I've got to ferry to the afterlife today? Pick up the pace!"

Aqua leaned back in her chair, not even looking at me as she spoke. She was shoving some little snack in her mouth...

This girl! She meets someone for the first time, and what does she do? Make fun of how they died! She thinks she can do whatever she wants just because she's kind of cute...

Naturally, her attitude made me pretty ticked off.

So she wanted me to hurry up and decide?

Fine, I'd decide.

Any one "thing" I wanted to take with me, right?

"...You, then." I pointed at Aqua.

Aqua looked at me blankly and put another snack in her mouth.

"Hmm. Okay, stay inside this magic circle..."

Suddenly, she caught herself.

"W-wait. What did you say?"

At that moment...

"Your wish is received. Then, Lady Aqua, I shall tend to your duties henceforth."

A winged woman appeared out of nowhere in a bright flash of light. She looked like some kind of angel.

"...What?" Aqua said stupidly. A blue magic circle appeared at her feet, and at mine.

Ooh, cool effects. Were we really headed to another world?

"Wait—what?! Y-you've gotta be kidding me! That wish doesn't count, right? No way it counts! Wait! Waiiit!" She flailed ineffectually, tears flying from her eyes.

"Safe travels, milady," the angel said to her. "Leave things to me. Whensoever you do defeat the Demon King, I shall send someone to retrieve you. Until then, allow me to attend to your duties."

"Wait! Seriously, wait! I'm a goddess! I can heal people, but I don't know how to fight! How am I supposed to defeat the Demon King?!"

The angel only glanced at the sobbing, prostrate Aqua, then gave me a gentle smile.

"Mr. Kazuma Satou. I will now send you to this new world, as one of the candidates for the hero who will defeat the Demon King. Whensoever you should do so, you will receive a gift from the gods."

"A gift…?" I asked.

"Yes. One commensurate with the worth of a world saved. The gods will grant any one thing you should ask."

"Cool!"

If I ended up getting sick of this new place, I could ask to go back to Japan, for example—

If I ended up getting sick of this new place, I could ask to go back to Japan, be filthy rich and surrounded by beautiful women, and spend the rest of my life playing video games! Just how decadent could a wish get?

"Hey, wait! That's a great line—and it's supposed to be mine!" It was Aqua again, bewailing the sudden loss of her job to this angel who'd come out of nowhere.

Frankly, I was rather pleased to see her like that. I pointed at Aqua.

"How does it feel to be dragged off to another world by the guy you were just making fun of? You're the one 'thing' I'm bringing along—so you'd better use that goddess power of yours to make my life as cushy as I want!"

"Noooo! Pleeease don't make me go to a new world with a man like this!!"

"Hero! I pray for your success as the one candidate of many who will bring low the Demon King. Now—hie you hence!"

The angel's solemn invocation was disturbed only by Aqua's cry:

"Nooooo! That's myyy liiiine, tooooo!"

Then the still-weeping Aqua and I were enveloped in a brilliant light...

Chapter 1

May I Go to a New World With This Self-Proclaimed Goddess!

1

Horse-drawn carriages rattled along the stone-paved streets of a town.

"It's…it's a parallel universe. Look around! We're in an actual other world! Am I really here? Am I really gonna get to learn magic and go adventuring?!"

I took in the scene before me, quivering with excitement.

Brick buildings stood eave to eave, like a scene straight from Middle Ages Europe.

There were no cars or motorcycles, no utility poles, no cell phone towers.

"Oh man! Ohhh man! Ohmanohmanohman!"

My eyes darted everywhere, watching the people passing by.

"He's got animal ears—real ones! And there's an elf! A real elf! She's gotta be an elf—she's so beautiful! Good-bye, modern-day hermit life! Hello, fantasy world! Now, this is a place where I could see actually going outside…getting a job and stop being a NEET—"

"Waaaaaaaaah! Waaaaaaaaaaaaaah! Waaaaaaaaaaaaaaaaaaaaaaah!"

I looked at Aqua, who was on her knees beside me, head in her hands.

*   *   *

"Hey, keep it down. What'll happen if everyone thinks I'm friends with a crazy lady? Anyway, don't you have something to give me right about now? I mean, look how I'm dressed. I'm wearing a tracksuit! In a fantasy world! If this was a game, I'd at least get some kind of basic starting equipment."

"Waaaaaaaaaaaaaaaaaaaaaaaaaaaaaaaaaaaaaaaaaaaaaaaaaaaaaaaaahhhh!!"

The goddess grabbed hold of me as she cried.

"Wh-whoa! What're you doing?! Stop it! I get it; I'll handle the starter gear myself! I mean—I'm sorry! If you hate it that much here, then fine—go home. I'll manage somehow."

My hands brushed Aqua's as I tried to free my neck from her grip.

To my surprise, her hands were shaking.

"What are you talking about?!" She wept, holding her head and dancing back and forth. "I *can't* go home—that's the problem! What am I gonna do? Arrrgh, come on! What am I supposed to do now?!"

She shook her waist-length hair, and I realized she would be a real beauty if she'd just shut up…but as it was, she came across as a diva. Frankly, I could barely bring myself to look at her.

"Hey, goddess, calm down. At times like this, you have to find the tavern. Start there, gather information. That's how role-playing games work."

"Wh—? I thought you were supposed to be some shut-in video game *otaku*. When did you get so reliable? By the way, Kazuma, my name is Aqua. It's sweet of you to call me 'goddess,' but you should probably use my name while we're here. If people knew who I really am, we might attract a crowd, and then how would we get to the Demon King? This may be a different world, but I am actually worshipped here."

With that, Aqua pattered along behind me. I, for my part, was feeling quite confident.

*   *   *

Now, there had to be a group of adventurers resisting the Demon King, or an Adventurers Guild that handled fighting monsters, or something.

Actually, come to think of it—Aqua's a goddess. Why not ask her?

"Aqua, how about an Adventurers Guild? Know where it is?" I said, but she just stared at me blankly.

"Sorry? I'm sure I don't know. I know only the most basic things about this world, not every little detail of its towns. Think about it—this is just one world among millions, and this town is just one insignificant settlement out of all the towns in this world. Why *should* I know anything about it?"

This girl is totally useless.

The conversation wasn't getting us anywhere, so I stopped a middle-aged woman on the street. It was better than asking a guy, who might've turned out to be trouble, or asking a young girl—my anxiety would've driven the difficulty of *that* "quest" through the roof.

"Excuse me, ma'am. May I ask you something? Is there anything like an Adventurers Guild around?"

"A guild? You mean you don't know? You must be new here." I relaxed at her words, knowing there had to be a guild here somewhere.

"Yes, ma'am. We've come from quite a ways off. We just arrived a little while ago."

"Oh my… If you've come to this town, you must be looking to become adventurers. Welcome to Axel, the town for novice adventurers. If you follow that street and turn right, you'll see a sign."

"Straight, then right. Thank you very much, ma'am! …Okay, we're off!"

The town for novice adventurers, huh?

A starter town. The ideal starting point for new, freshly dead arrivals from some other world.

After thanking the woman and heading down the road she'd pointed out, I could feel Aqua looking at me with new respect as she darted along behind me.

"Hey," she said with a hint of astonishment, "how'd you come up with that story on the spot? You actually seem quite capable. So then why were you a hermit of an *otaku* who'd never had a girlfriend or really any friends at all? Why spend your days as a hikiNEET?"

"Not having friends or a girlfriend isn't necessarily a bad thing. You can't judge a person's worth by how many friends they have or if they're in a relationship. And don't call me a hikiNEET, you dumb bimbo. Don't assume all *hikikomori* are NEETs. I was just sixteen. That's too young for society to assume I'll be a member of the workforce… Ah, there it is."

Aqua made to strangle me at the words *dumb bimbo*, but I ignored her and went into the Adventurers Guild.

—Adventurers Guild—

You'll find an Adventurers Guild in every video game. It's an organization that helps adventurers find work or otherwise supports them. It's basically a fantasy-world version of Hello Work, that government employment service.

The Guild was housed in a fairly large building, and the smell of food drifted from within.

There was a rough lot inside, no doubt. People who might not think twice about jumping some newcomers.

I steeled myself for conflict as I entered…

…and was greeted by a waitress with short red hair, who said sweetly, "Oh, welcome! If you're looking for work, go to the counter inside. If you're here for a meal, please take any open seat."

The dim interior looked to be home to a tavern.

People in armor wandered here and there, but no one seemed especially out to cause trouble.

We did seem to be getting a lot of attention, though. At first I thought maybe they didn't get many newcomers here.

Then it dawned on me.

"Hey, I don't like the way they're looking at me," Aqua said. "I know! It's the goddess aura I exude—they've figured out who I really am!"

Everyone was checking out the goddess who stood beside me, spewing inanities. It made sense that she would attract attention. After all, she would be really beautiful, if she could keep her mouth shut.

I decided to ignore the stares and pursue my original objective.

"Listen, Aqua. Once we register, the Guild will give us some tutorials, teaching us how to survive as new adventurers. They should lend us enough money to go on an adventure and get us work that'll keep food on the table even though we're just starting out. Maybe they'll let us know where the best inns are. Most games start this way. Normally I'd say it was your job to make sure we had the basic necessities for life in this world, but…never mind. Today, let's just get registered, make sure we've got enough money for starter equipment, and find somewhere to sleep."

"I don't know what you're talking about. *My job* is to send dead people to this world. But, fine. I don't know anything about video games, but I take it this is how you get started in this kind of world. I just have to register as an adventurer, right?"

"That's right. Let's go!"

I pulled Aqua along toward the counter.

There were four receptionists.

Two were women.

I went to the prettier of the two.

"Hey, we could've gone to any of the other three and not had to wait in line," Aqua said from behind me. "Why'd you pick this one? Wait, I get it. It's because she's the prettiest, isn't it? Sheesh, just when I think maybe I can count on you for something…"

She doesn't know anything. I turned to her and said in a whisper, "Lesson one, be on good terms with the girl at the Guild. Lesson two, the pretty ones always have a backstory. There's gotta be an event flag waiting. Someday we'll find out that girl used to be a renowned hunter or something."

"Come to think of it, I've seen that sort of thing in comic books, too. Sorry. I'll just stand in line here."

The receptionists at the open windows all glared at us for deliberately lining up at this one, but I ignored them.

Finally it was our turn.

"Hello, how can I help you today?" The receptionist seemed very gentle and was certainly very beautiful. Her wavy hair and generous bosom gave her a mature look.

"Um, we'd like to become adventurers, but we just got here from the countryside and don't have any idea what to do…"

If I dropped in a bit about being from the sticks or some other land, the receptionist would presumably take the initiative to tell us what we needed to know.

"I see… Well, a registration fee is required. Will that be all right?"

There you go. A tutorial, just like that.

Now we just had to do what she'd told us, and…

…Registration fee?

"…Hey, Aqua, you got any cash?"

"What do you think? As if I had time to grab my wallet when you dragged me off here!"

What were we going to do? Maybe we could get a loan for starters, or postpone the fee?

Aqua and I stepped away from the window to plan our strategy.

"What're we gonna do now? We've been at this for five minutes and we've already hit a roadblock! In a game, you usually just start with some basic equipment, or at least a little money."

"Gosh, what happened to that manly confidence you had a few

minutes ago? Oh well, I guess it can't be helped. You *are* a *hikikomori.* Fine, my turn. You just watch. I'll show you what it means to be a goddess."

A man was sitting nearby in what seemed to be priest's vestments, ratty and worn though they were. Aqua boldly strode up to him.

"You, priest! State your denomination! I am Aqua! Yes, Aqua, she who is venerated by the Church of Axis! If you be among my followers......it would...really help if you could...lend me some money."

I couldn't tell if she was commanding or begging.

"I'm afraid I'm of the Eris sect..."

"Oh, is that so? Sorry to bother you, then..."

I guess he wasn't one of her followers.

Aqua turned dejectedly and made to leave, but the priest called out to her.

"Oh, miss...! You're a follower of the Axis sect? In the old stories, the goddesses Aqua and Eris were said to be senior and junior to each other. It must be fate that brought you to me. I saw you didn't have enough money to pay the registration fee. Here, let me give you enough for that. Call it Eris's blessing. But, miss—however devoted a follower you may be, you shouldn't call yourself a goddess!"

"Oh...right. Sorry. Thank you very much..."

Aqua took the money and came back, wearing a look that reminded me of a dead fish.

"Ha-ha... He didn't even believe I was a goddess... You know, Eris is my junior. I got money because the follower of an under-goddess of mine took pity on me..."

"W-well, hey—all's well that ends well, right? It would've been a problem if he *had* believed you, wouldn't it?" Aqua looked like she'd lost something important, and I wanted to say something encouraging.

"Um, ma'am, we've...got the registration fee."

"Uh...huh. That will be one thousand eris each, please."

The priest had given Aqua three thousand eris. According to Aqua, one eris was roughly equal to one yen, so he'd basically given her three thousand yen.

The girl at the window hadn't said anything about our little display with the priest. In fact, she seemed to hardly want to look at us. *So much for lesson one.*

"Now, you've said you want to become adventurers, so I assume you have some idea of what's involved. But just in case, please allow me to explain. First of all, adventurers are those who fight the monsters—that is, creatures who do harm to people—outside town. However, they are also jacks-of-all-trades. *Adventurer* is simply a generic term for those who have accepted this life as their vocation. Each one also has an occupation."

There it was! Finally!

This was what defined an adventurer. Call it an occupation, a job, a class—this was where we got to choose our fighting style.

Forget being some run-of-the-mill warrior. A good, flashy spell-caster class was in my future.

The receptionist set a card in front of me and another in front of Aqua. It was about the size of a driver's license—presumably some kind of identification.

"You see the line marked *level*? As you know, every creature in this world has a soul within it. Whenever we eat or kill or otherwise end the life of another living thing, we absorb some portion of its memories. The memories we absorb are widely known as *experience points*. Typically, you can't see them. However…"

She pointed to another part of the card.

"…this section will show an adventurer how many experience points he or she has gained. The corresponding level will be shown, too. So the card's a guidepost to an adventurer's strength and also indicates how many monsters he or she has defeated. Any living thing, once it gains enough experience, will suddenly and dramatically grow in its abilities. People often describe this as reaching a new plateau or, in a word, *leveling up*… At any rate, when your level goes up, you gain points, which you can spend on new skills as well as a variety of other benefits. So make sure to work hard and raise your level."

That reminded me of what Aqua had said.

You like video games, right?

Now it made sense. Everything the girl just explained was straight out of an RPG.

"I'd like you both to fill out this form. Please give your height, weight, age, and distinctive physical features."

I began to write on the form she handed me. Height, five foot four; weight, a hundred and twenty pounds. Sixteen years old, brown hair, brown eyes…

"All right, thank you. Now, each of you—please touch these cards. They will show your stats so you can pick a class that matches your abilities. Based on that class, you may also be able to learn specialized skills at higher levels, so consider that when deciding on your occupation."

Ooh, that was quick.

This was where my incredible latent abilities would become evident—no doubt the entire Guild Hall would be in an uproar. I touched the card with a mixture of trepidation and excitement.

"…All right, thank you. Mr.…Kazuma Satou, is that right? Let's see… Strength, Vitality, Magic, Agility…all average. Your Intelligence is on the high side… Huh? Your Luck is extremely high. Though Luck isn't a very useful stat for adventurers, I'm afraid… What should we do? With these stats, you can't actually specialize. You'll have to choose the basic Adventurer class. With your Luck, I might even recommend you give up adventuring and become a merchant instead… Would you like to do that?"

Wait, did I just get rejected *as an adventurer? What's this about?*

It was all I could do not to smack the snickering goddess beside me.

If I was weak, it would be as much a problem for her as for me.

"F-fine, just…Adventurer then, please."

"W-well," the girl said with a worried look, "as your level goes up, your stats will improve, and you can eventually change jobs! And—notice how the Adventurer class shares its name with the word that refers to everyone who goes on adventures? It's a sort of general occupation. Just because it's a starter class doesn't mean it's bad. People with the Adventurer job can learn and use skills from any class!"

"The trade-off is that skills take tons of points to learn, and you can't expect them to be anywhere near as effective as when someone of the proper class uses them. Jack-of-all-trades, master of none!" Leave it to Aqua to rain on my parade.

I wondered if I could just lose her somewhere.

Anyway, starter class or "general occupation," it looked like I was stuck as an Adventurer. The weakest class of all.

But it didn't matter. The weakest adventurer was still an adventurer, and I was just as poised to take on a world out of my video games. It was with no small stirring of my heart that I took the card with my name and the word ADVENTURER…

"Wh—whaaaat?! Where did these numbers come from?! Besides your below-average Intelligence and your abysmal Luck, all your stats are vastly above average! Your Magic is the most amazing of all! Who or what are you, ma'am?!" The receptionist could barely contain herself as she looked at Aqua's card.

The building filled with excited murmurs.

Wait, wasn't that supposed to happen for *me*?

"R-really? S-so I'm amazing or something? Well, I guess I *am* me, after all…"

She might be obnoxious, but she was still a goddess.

Even so, it was hard not to hate her as she grew more and more pleased with her stats.

"*A-amazing* doesn't begin to cover it! You can't pick the Wizard class, which requires high Intelligence, but…you can be anything else at all!

You could be a Crusader—a Knight famed for impenetrable defense—or you could be a Sword Master, with unparalleled attack power! You could be an Arch-priest, the most advanced of the Priest classes. You can *start* in some of the most advanced occupations available!"

Aqua seemed to mull that over.

"I see, I see… It's just a shame *goddess* isn't a class. Well, maybe Arch-priest would be right for me, then."

"Arch-priest it is! A very versatile class, with all types of healing and support spells, but also strong enough to stand fearlessly at the front line! Let's see…Arch-priest… There. Welcome to the Adventurers Guild, honored Aqua! I and the entire staff look forward to your future exploits!"

The girl at the desk had a huge smile on her face.

…What is going on here? Seriously, am I the main character or not?

Well, never mind.

And this was how my life as an adventurer in a new world began.

2

"All riiiight—good work, everyone! That's it for today! Here, come and get your pay!"

"Thank you, sir! Another good day of work, sir!"

"Whooo, work!"

At the foreman's announcement of the end of the workday, Aqua and I each offered a word of thanks and a bow of the head.

"Okay, everyone," I said. "See you tomorrow!"

"Whooo, tomorrow!" Aqua echoed as I said good-bye to the other workers.

"Right, good work! And tomorrow's another day!" With the others' voices still in our ears, Aqua and I walked off the site.

Phew! Another day's work finished.

Even I could hardly believe I was once a *hikikomori*. Aqua and I headed for the town's largest public bath, clutching our day's wages.

The baths here were more or less the same as the ones in Japan. The entry fee was maybe a bit higher compared to the average wage, but a hot bath after a long day of work was something I couldn't let fall by the wayside, even if it was a little expensive.

"Awww, yeah… That's the stuff…"

I sank into the steaming bath up to my shoulders, letting the water wash away the day's fatigue.

This world looked a bit like the Middle Ages, and I'd always assumed baths would be a luxury in a fantasy world, but apparently I'd been wrong.

And thank goodness…!

Aqua left the bath and waited for me at the entrance. I guess it's not very chivalrous to make a woman wait while you finish soaking, but then again, maybe that's just a bath-loving Japanese person for you.

"What do you wanna eat today? I want a Smoke Lizard burger. And a nice cold Crimson Neroid!"

"Yeah, I'd like some meat, too. Well, how about we get the guy at the inn to whip us up a couple of his Smoke Lizard hamburger combo meals?"

"No objections!"

Aqua and I wolfed down our meals, and then, with nothing special to do, we went back to the stable we were staying at.

I picked the hay that smelled the least like horse poop to make my bed and lay right down. Aqua was curled up nearby as though it were the most natural thing in the world.

"'Kay, g'night!"

"…Night. Man, we really did some work today…"

And so I began to drift off into a deep, satisfied sl…

"Wait, hold on a minute!"

I bolted upright.

"What's wrong? Did you forget to use the toilet before bed? It's dark outside. Want me to go with you?"

"No! That's not it. Why are we doing manual labor every day?"

Yes.

Aqua and I had spent every day of the last two weeks working on an expansion to the town wall. I.e., doing construction work.

This was a far cry from the adventuring I'd expected when I came here.

Come to think of it, how had Aqua adapted so uncomplainingly to this life?

She's a goddess, isn't she?

"Well, it's 'cause if you want to eat, you have to work. Don't you like construction? Sheesh. This is why you're a hikiNEET. You could hawk goods in the shopping district, if you'd rather?"

"That's not the point! I want— I came here for heart-pounding battles with monsters, okay? I thought the Demon King's invasion was threatening this place! But you couldn't *find* a more peaceful world! There's no demons; there's hardly any kings—what did we come here for?!"

Our voices got louder as our tempers flared, until we heard shouts nearby:

"Hey, you! Shaddup! People are tryin' to sleep!"

"Oh! Sorry! So sorry…"

Novice adventurers are poor, okay? They don't have the money for a room at the inn every night. Usually they pool their resources with other adventurers and sleep in one big dormitory-style room, but right now, all we could afford to rent was a haystack in the stables.

Yeah…definitely not living up to how I'd envisioned the adventuring life in a fantasy world.

Staying at the inn was sort of like if you slept in a hotel every night back in Japan. Not a lifestyle for those without a steady income—like us, for example.

Video games normally feature some simple starter quests, like harvesting herbs or hunting some monsters near town. No such thing here. Plus, monsters don't just spew money when you defeat them, either.

The monsters that lived in the forest near town had been wiped out long ago. And who'd pay money for someone to gather herbs in a perfectly peaceful forest?

No one, obviously.

Even children left the town's walls with impunity. There was a guard at the gate, sure, but not the kind who locks everything down so tight an ant could hardly get in. The forest wasn't big enough to be that worrisome—if anything dangerous showed up, the people just went out and got rid of it.

I guess it made sense when you thought about it, but it was all a bit too real-world-y for my liking.

In a game, a fresh-faced adventurer could go out in the woods, spend half a day picking easily distinguishable plants and herbs, and make enough money to pay for three square meals and a soft bed, too.

But when in real life has there ever been such easy money?

Think about it. Even in a rich country like Japan, have you ever met a laborer who spends every day of his life in a decent hotel?

Minimum wage? Labor laws? What are those? Are they tasty?

Welcome to your RPG fantasy.

"I—I know all that. This is the farthest town from the Demon King's castle. He'd never bother attacking all the way out here, especially a town with nothing but greenhorns. So, Kazuma, you're telling me you want to go on a real adventure? Before you've even gotten any gear together?"

In the face of Aqua's blunt analysis, there was nothing I could say.

It was true. Aqua and I lacked even the most basic provisions for adventuring. We'd taken our nice, safe construction jobs in hopes of saving up enough to buy some equipment.

"I'm getting pretty tired of construction... I didn't come all the way to a land of swords and sorcery just to work with my hands. I came here to adventure—no computers or game consoles needed. I was sent here to drive out the Demon King, wasn't I?"

For a moment, Aqua looked at me as though she couldn't understand what I was talking about. Then she exclaimed, "Oh, that's right! We did mean to do something like that, didn't we? I got so caught up in the joy of work that I completely forgot, but if you don't take out the Demon King, I can't go home, can I?"

I was a bit taken aback by her words, until I recalled the receptionist's remark that Aqua's Intelligence stat was below average.

"Fine, let's go take him out! You've got me with you, so we'll be fiiiine. You can count on me!"

"I've got a bad feeling about this… But I guess you *are* a goddess. All right, it's up to you! Tomorrow we'll get the cheapest equipment we can find and then start working on our levels!"

"Just leave it to me!"

"I thought I told you to shaddup! Don't make me come over there!"

"Sorry! Pardon us!"

Even as we apologized to the other adventurer, my heart was dancing in my chest, and soon I was asleep.

3

There wasn't a cloud in the bright blue sky.

"Aaaaaaaaaaaaaahhh! Help me! Aqua, help meee!"

"Pffft! Hee-hee-hee! This is great! Kazuma, your face is so red! The tears, the desperation—I love it!"

Right. I'll bury her in the ground on my way home.

Even as I plotted to leave Aqua in the dirt, I ran around screaming for her help as the Giant Toad, a massive frog-like monster, chased me.

We were in the vast field surrounding the town.

This was where grabbing a quest at the Guild had gotten us…

I had a short sword, the most minimal of weaponry. Aqua, for her part, had said some dumb thing about how a goddess waving a sword just wouldn't look right, and so she was currently without any weapon at all. Instead, she gaily watched the toad chase me around.

I guess you can't underestimate your enemy, even when he's a frog.

These frogs—sorry, toads—were bigger than cows. During mating season, they needed strength to lay their eggs and so would migrate to human towns, where there was plenty of food...as in the local farmers' goats, which the toads would swallow whole.

Since Aqua and I hardly weighed more than a couple of goats ourselves, we were both pretty concerned by this revelation. As a matter of fact, it turned out that every year, around Giant Toad mating season, a number of farmers and even children would go missing from the town.

On the outside, these monsters looked just like huge frogs. But they were far more dangerous than the weaklings that had been cleared out of the area so long ago.

Incidentally, their meat, while a little tough, was light and mild-tasting and was considered a delicacy.

We'd heard that their thick layer of fat protected them from physical attacks. Then again, we'd also heard that because Giant Toads hate metal, if you wore even just a tiny bit of armor you could avoid being eaten, so they weren't so hard to deal with after all. That's why experienced adventurers enjoyed hunting them. We, however...

"Aqua! Aqua!! Don't just stand there laughing—help meee!"

"Maybe you could start by showing me a bit of respect."

"*Lady* Aquaaaaa!"

I'd get her later. Bury her up to her neck and leave her there so *she* knew how scary it was to be at the mercy of a Giant Toad. Nearly in tears, I glanced back at the creature pursuing me. But it had turned away from me. It was looking at…

"Well, all right! I guess I have to help you out, then, you hikiNEET.

In return, I expect you to worship me—starting tomorrow! When we get back to town, you have to join the Axis Church and pray to me three times a day! At meals, if I ask for something on your plate, you have to give it to me without complaint! And— Hrgh?!"

Aqua and all her self-aggrandizing suddenly vanished.

The Giant Toad that had been chasing me had stopped moving. From one corner of its mouth, something blue was sprouting.

It was…

"Aqua! H-hey, don't you dare get eaten!"

Aqua's leg hung out the side of the frog's mouth, shaking.

I drew my short sword—and leaped at the Giant Toad!

"*Sniffle*… Waaaaah! *Sniff*…"

Aqua squatted on the ground in front of me, hugging her knees. She was dripping with slime.

Next to her lay the Giant Toad, its head split open.

"*Sniff…sniff…* Th-thank you, Kazuma… Thank you…! Waaaaaaaaaaaahhhh!!"

She hadn't stopped crying since I'd pulled her from the toad's mouth.

I guess even goddesses don't like being eaten.

"I-it's all right, Aqua. Take it easy… Hey, let's go home for today. The quest was to kill five toads in three days, but we're obviously in over our heads. Let's get some more gear first. I mean, I've got a short sword and a tracksuit… I'd at least like to *look* like an adventurer."

I'd been able to kill the toad that swallowed Aqua mainly because Giant Toads stop moving when they swallow their prey. I never would have had the guts to go up against a toad that was happily hopping toward me to attack.

But Aqua, her whole body covered in gleaming toad mucus, rose to her feet.

"*Sniff*... How can a goddess just allow herself to be brought down to this level by some frog? I've been defiled! If one of my followers saw me now, they'd lose all faith in me! If it got out that I'd been laid low by a *frog*, the reputation of the beautiful and awesome Aqua would be for naught!"

She sweat every day as she lugged around construction loads, thrilled to be able to carry more than a bunch of middle-aged men. She looked forward to nothing more than dinner after a good bath. Every night she slept next to me on a hay bale, drool dribbling down her chin... But cover her in a little frog slime, and *now* she worried about appearances?

Before I could stop her, Aqua dashed off toward another Giant Toad in the distance.

"Whoa! Hey, wait—Aqua!"

She ignored me, closing the gap between her and the monster. With all the energy that propelled her, her fist began to emit a white light, and she slammed it into the toad's belly.

"Know the power of the gods! You shouldn't have stood against me—and bared your fangs against us—but you'll have time to regret that in Hell! *God Blow*!"

I recalled hearing from a Guild employee that physical attacks weren't all that effective against Giant Toads.

Aqua's fist sank into the monster's soft stomach with a *glug*, and the toad casually looked down at her...

Aqua met his eyes. "Y-you know, now that I see you up close, I r-realize how cute Giant Toads really are..."

For the second time that day, I set upon a monster immobilized while eating its meal, and for the second time, I rescued a sobbing, slime-covered goddess.

We decided to call it a day.

4

"The problem is, the two of us alone are totally outmatched. We need some allies!"

When we got back to town, we'd gone directly to the bathhouse. Then we'd headed to the Adventurers Guild, where we were eating fried frog legs and holding a war council.

The Guild Hall functioned as both an adventurers' meeting place and a recreation facility. You could buy and sell monster parts, and a large tavern served up monster-based dishes.

We'd gotten two frogs' worth of meat today, which we sold to the Guild for some pocket change.

We could hardly carry back those carcasses ourselves. But the Guild offered a transport service—for a price. Minus the transport fee, we earned five thousand eris for each frog. All told, it was barely more than we'd been making in construction.

Then again, the fried frog—while a little tough—was way better than I'd expected. When I first got to this world, I'd been loath to eat things like lizards or frogs, but it turned out they were pretty good in a combo meal.

The goddess sitting across from me, though, didn't need any encouragement to eat everything that was put in front of her.

"Sure, but…we're brand-new adventurers who don't even have any decent gear. What kind of 'allies' would join our party?"

Aqua waved her fork back and forth, her mouth full of frog leg.

"Doan' worry abouf it! I'm the one whof'll be recruifing!"

"Swallow first! Swallow first, then talk!"

She gulped down her mouthful of food. "*I'm* here. When word gets out we want party members, they'll come. I am an Arch-priest, you know—an advanced class! I can use all kinds of healing magic; I can cure paralysis and poisoning, even revive the dead! What party *wouldn't* want me? I might not have anywhere near my full power, thanks to you dragging me down to the mortal realm, but— Ahem! I'm the great Aqua, aren't I? Pretty soon they'll be knocking at our door. 'Please let us join you!' they'll say. Get it? Now, pass me another fried frog leg."

With that, she grabbed a leg off my plate, and I looked at this self-proclaimed goddess with a sinking feeling.

5

At the Adventurers Guild the next day:

"………Where *are* they?" Aqua groaned.

We'd posted a notice that we were seeking party members and then set up shop at a table in a far corner of the Guild Hall…but so far we'd been sitting here for more than half the day, and not one candidate for "Future Hero" had shown up.

Maybe no one had seen our posting.

There were lots of other adventurers looking for party members. But they seemed to have one interview after another and then, after a friendly chat, would go off somewhere with their new ally.

I knew why no one was coming to our table.

"Maybe we need to lower our standards a little. I get that we're trying to defeat the Demon King here, but the part that says, 'Only those of advanced classes need apply' is probably putting people off."

"Uhh… But… But…"

The class system in this fantasy world included what were called "advanced classes." Aqua's class, Arch-priest, was an example. It was a stage normal people would never reach—heroes of legend, if you will. And obviously, most everyone with that kind of talent had already found parties…

Aqua was probably just looking to get the most powerful people we could to help us take on the Demon King. But…

"At this rate, no one's going to show up. Anyway, you might be an advanced class, but I have the lowest job there is. How can I hold my head up if my entire party's full of elite characters? Let's cast a wider net, please?" As I spoke, I made to stand up. But then…

"I saw the notice seeking adventurers of advanced classes. Is this the right place?"

I met a red eye that looked oddly languid, almost sleepy. Full black hair that just barely reached the shoulders.

The girl who'd spoken to us was the very image of a spell-caster: black mantle and black robe, black boots, a staff, even a pointy hat. She had doll-like features—one of those "Lolita" types.

I knew it wasn't unusual in this world for children to work, but this girl couldn't have been more than twelve or thirteen. She was short and wore a patch over one eye, and suddenly she threw back her mantle and declared: "I am Megumin! I am of the occupation Arch-wizard, one who wields the most powerful of all offensive magics, Explosion!"

"...Are you messing with us?"

"I—I am not!"

She didn't seem to expect me to dismiss her self-introduction.

And what was with that name, anyway?

"...That red eye. Are you one of the Crimson Magic Clan?"

The girl nodded at Aqua's question and passed her Adventurer's Card to Aqua.

"Indeed I am! I am Megumin, first among the spell-casters of the Crimson Magic Clan! My ultimate magic can level mountains and shatter stone...! Y-you don't happen to need an exceptional magic-user, do you? ...And if you will pardon my asking, could you give me something to eat before we start the interview? I haven't had a bite to eat in three days..." She looked at us pleadingly.

At the same moment, her stomach gave a loud gurgle.

"I don't mind treating you," I said. "But what's with the eye patch? If you're injured, Aqua here can fix you up."

"...Heh. This is a magic item that restrains my incredible power. If I removed it...why, then a great calamity would come upon this world..."

"Wow, really? So it's like some kind of seal?"

"Oh, no, I made all that up just now. I just think it looks cool... Ow! I'm sorry! Stop! Please don't pull on it!"

"All right, let me fill in Kazuma," Aqua said as I tugged on Megumin's

eye patch. "These kids, the Crimson Magic Clan, are born with exceptionally high Intelligence and Magic, making it easy for them to become expert spell-casters. They're distinguished by their red eyes, which give them their name and...well, their weird personal names."

Huh. I'd thought she was just teasing me about the eye patch and the name.

I let the patch go, and Megumin collected herself.

"Weird names, indeed! From my perspective it is everyone else in town who has a weird name."

"...Out of curiosity, what were your parents' names?"

"My mother is Yuiyui. My father, Hyoizaburou!"

Aqua and I looked at her in silence.

"...Well, anyway. You said this kid's people turn out a lot of great magic-users? How about we take her, then?"

"Hey! If you have something to say about my parents' names, let us hear it!" Megumin shoved her face up close to mine. Aqua quickly returned her Adventurer's Card.

"Why not? You can't forge an Adventurer's Card, and this girl's definitely an Arch-wizard, an advanced class capable of powerful offensive magic. If she really can use Explosion, that would be a big deal. That's supposed to be among the most difficult magic to master."

"Hey," Megumin said hotly, "you do not have to call me *this girl* all the time. Use my name."

I passed her a menu. "Calm down and order something. I'm Kazuma. This is Aqua. Pleasure to meet you, Arch-wizard."

Megumin looked like she was about to say something, then silently took the menu.

6

"Explosion is the most powerful of magics. But it takes time to prepare in proportion to its power. I will need you to hold that toad at bay until I am ready."

Aqua, the now-sated Megumin, and I had come to get some revenge on the Giant Toads.

We could see one of them far off across the field. It had noticed us and was coming closer. But we could also see other toads approaching from the opposite direction.

"Use your magic to target the one that's farther away. As for the closer ones…well, here we go, Aqua. Time to get our payback. You keep telling me you used to be a—y'know. Why don't you show me what you can do?"

"What do you mean, *used to be*?! It's present tense: I *am* a goddess! I'm just an Arch-priest for now!"

Megumin gave the self-proclaimed goddess a strange look as Aqua strangled me with tears flying from her eyes.

"A…goddess?"

"…I-is what she calls herself! Poor kid. Sometimes she just lets it slip, you know? Don't pay her any attention." As I spoke, Megumin looked sympathetically at Aqua.

The tearful Aqua made a fist and lunged desperately at the nearest frog.

"Whatever! I know Giant Toads are supposed to be resistant to physical attacks, but this time I'm going to show you what a goddess can do! Just you watch, Kazuma! I didn't get my glory last time, but today—!"

With that, Aqua, who seemed to have learned nothing from her previous foray into a frog's digestive system, ceased to move and stalled the Giant Toad in her own way.

Only a true goddess would sacrifice herself to buy her allies some time!

That was when the air around Megumin began to tremble.

Even I, who didn't know the first thing about magic, could see that what Megumin was cooking up was serious stuff. Her voice grew louder as she chanted the incantation, and a single bead of sweat rolled down her forehead.

"Behold! The most powerful magic known to mankind! This is truly the ultimate attack magic!"

The end of Megumin's staff began to glow. The vast light condensed until it was tiny but piercingly bright. Megumin's red eye glowed as she opened it wide.

"*Explosion*!!"

A single beam of light flew across the field. It raced from the end of her staff and enveloped the frog that was coming in our direction.

Then I saw the effect of this dire magic.

The frog burst into tiny pieces with a light bright enough to set your head spinning and a roar that shook the air. I planted my feet and covered my eyes against a shock wave that threatened to send me flying. When the smoke cleared, a twenty-meter-wide crater lay where the creature had been, speaking to the awesomeness of the blast.

"In-*cred*-ible! So this is magic…" At that moment, while I was admiring Megumin's spell, a Giant Toad—perhaps awakened by the sound and the shock wave—crawled up from under the ground.

I'd been wondering how the toads survived in an area without rainfall or a major water source, but I'd never thought they might do it by living underground.

The toad was crawling out near Megumin but moving very slowly.

I just had to get her back far enough to prepare another explosion.

"Megumin! Let's fall back, then we can hit them agai—"

That was as far as I got before I saw Megumin…and stopped in my tracks.

She had collapsed.

"M-my magic is utterly powerful, b-but it takes strength e-equal to its power… I've overexerted myself and w-will not be moving for a while… Oh, who could have known a toad would appear right near me? This is trouble. I shall be eaten. P-please help— Mfffgh?!"

I finished off the two toads Megumin and Aqua had immobilized. And so it was that we did actually kill five Giant Toads in three days…

Quest successful.

7

"*Sniffle…sniffle…* It stinks… My clothes stiiink…!"

A whimpering, slime-covered Aqua trudged behind me.

"The inside of a Giant Toad smells bad, but it's rather cozy and warm. Add that to the list of things I never really wanted to know first-hand." The equally slime-covered Megumin was perched on my back, offering up facts I myself didn't really want to know.

It turns out that when a spell-caster uses a spell that goes beyond the limits of her MP, she makes up the difference out of her HP. Use a major spell when your mana is running low, and it could even put your life at risk.

"Save your explosions for emergencies from now on, Megumin," I said. "You should stick to smaller stuff most of the time."

I felt her hand, resting on my shoulder, clench. "I…can't."

"Huh?" I said dumbly. "You can't what?"

She gripped my shoulder even harder. I felt her small chest pressing against my back. "I can't…use anything but Explosion. I'm completely incapable of casting any other spells."

"…You're kidding."

"No, I am not."

Megumin and I fell silent. Aqua, who'd been quietly sniffling in the background the whole time, finally saw fit to enter the conversation.

"What do you mean, you can't use anything but Explosion? If you have enough skill points for that, surely you have enough to learn other spells, too?"

…Skill points?

Oh yeah—the girl at the Guild had said something about points being connected to learning skills. Aqua saw my expression and explained—

"You get skill points when you choose a class, and you use them to learn abilities. The better you are, the more points you start with, and you can allocate them to various skills. For example, I am *very* exceptional, so I started by learning all the party-trick skills and then all the magic appropriate to an Arch-priest."

"What are party-trick skills for?"

Aqua ignored my question.

"The types of skills a person can learn are limited by their class and personality," she went on. "For example, someone who hates water would have to spend more points to learn ice- or water-related skills or, in a worst-case scenario, might not be able to learn them at all. Explosive magics are part of the category called multi-type magic, because they rely on a deep knowledge of both fire and air magic, among others. Someone who can learn a spell from the explosive magics should have no problem learning other elemental magic."

"In other words, there's no reason you should be able to use an advanced spell like Explosion and not easier spells." I paused. "So. When and where does one use party-trick skills?"

From my back, Megumin whispered, "I…am an Arch-wizard who adores Explosion above all else. I do not care for all the explosive magics—Explosion is my only love."

I was starting to wonder what made Explosion different from any other "explosive magics."

I had no idea, but Aqua seemed to be taking Megumin's declaration of uniqueness quite seriously.

Actually, you know what? The thing about "party-trick skills" bugged me even more than the semantics of magically blowing stuff up.

"Of course it might be easier for me to go adventuring if I took other skills. Even abilities in the basic elements of fire, water, earth, and air would help me… But I cannot. I love only Explosion. Even if, with my present MP, I can cast it only once a day. Even if I collapse after casting it. It does not matter. I love only Explosion! Indeed, I chose the path of the Arch-wizard merely and solely so I could cast that one spell!"

"Incredible!" Aqua said. "Just wonderful! When I see you pursuing something so utterly impractical—and yet so romantic—I'm moved to tears…!"

Well, this was no good. Looked like this mage had decided to specialize in being useless. The ultimate proof was that *Aqua* sympathized with her.

Our recent battles with the Giant Toads had left me doubting whether this goddess was going to be any help to me at all. To be blunt, Aqua was a liability all by herself. To take on another problem child…

All right. I'd made up my mind.

"Wow, is that so?" I said. "Well, it won't be an easy road, but stay strong! Oh, hey, there's the town! When we get to the Guild, let's split the reward three ways. And then, who knows? Maybe we'll meet again someday…"

As I spoke, Megumin's grip on my shoulder tightened.

"Heh… My one desire is to let off Explosion. Any reward is merely a bonus. I do not need an equal share. Give me enough for a meal and a bath and some necessities, and I will ask nothing further. Yes! You can have me, an Arch-wizard, for hardly more than the price of a meal! Could you do anything other than take me on long-term under such conditions?"

"Ha-ha! Oh, we couldn't! Such phenomenal power would be wasted on a small-fry party like ours! Pearls before swine, you know? A regular spell-caster would be plenty for a couple of novices like us. Look at me—I'm the lowest possible class!"

As I spoke, I tried desperately to loosen Megumin's grip on my shoulder so I could send her on her way as soon as we reached the Guild Hall. Megumin tried desperately to hold on.

"Not at all! I don't mind in the least if this is a weak or inexperienced party. I may belong to an advanced class, but I am a novice myself. I am only Level 6! I am sure that with a few more levels I will stop collapsing every time I cast a spell. R-right? S-so please, s-stop trying to p-pull my hand away…"

"No, no, no. A spell-caster who can cast only one spell per day? That's hardly user-friendly. Oof! Wh-who'd have thought a mage could have such a strong grip...? Hey, leggo! You've probably been kicked out of other parties, too, haven't you? Think about it! If we go into a dungeon, you won't be able to use your Explosion in a confined space like that! You won't be able to help us at all! H-hey, let go already! Don't worry—we'll give you the reward from this quest! Now *let...go*!"

"Please don't abandon me! No other party will take me! When we go into a dungeon, I can...I can carry your bags for you! I'll do anything! I'm begging you, please don't leave me!"

Maybe it was the girl on my back shouting, "Please don't abandon me!" at the top of her lungs that attracted the looks and whispers of passersby. By now, we were already in town. Usually just Aqua alone was enough to gather a crowd, so we must have really stood out.

"Oh my goodness... That man is going to abandon that poor girl..."

"What's all over that woman next to him? Is that slime?"

"He made such a young girl his plaything—and now he's just going to throw her away? Disgusting! Look—both those girls are slimy! What kind of sick games was that perv playing with them?"

...I seemed to be the subject of a major misunderstanding.

I hated the way Aqua smirked when she heard those comments. And then it turned out Megumin had picked up on them, too.

As I looked over my shoulder at her, her mouth twisted, then opened...

"I'll play whatever games you want! I'll even put up with the slime play you showed me with those Giant Toads earlier!"

"All right, all right, enough! Welcome aboard, Megumin!"

8

"All right, I see you killed five Giant Toads within three days, as requested. The completion of your quest is confirmed. Good work, everyone!"

I made our report to the receptionist at the Adventurers Guild and received the posted reward.

Aqua and Megumin both stank of toad slime and might have caused more untoward misconceptions to boot, so I'd sent them off to the public bath.

I had been a little concerned about proving we'd killed all five toads, since one of them had been vaporized by a magical explosion, but it turned out my Adventurer's Card indicated how many monsters I'd killed and of what type. I presented my card to the receptionist along with Megumin's, and the girl simply used a strange box on the counter to check them.

It was true that magic rather than science had been the focus of development in this world, but there was still some pretty amazing technology here.

When I looked at my card again, it said ADVENTURER LEVEL 4.

I'd heard Giant Toads were an easy way for beginning adventurers to raise their level. I'd taken out four of them all by myself, and it had been enough to get me to Level 4. Then again, the lower your level, the quicker it went up. The stats on my card had risen a bit, but I didn't feel like I'd gotten especially stronger.

I found myself muttering, "So you really do get better just by defeating a few monsters…"

Back when she'd first introduced us to adventuring, the girl at the counter had told us that everything in this world had a soul. That whenever you eat something or kill something—whenever you put an end to the life of another living thing—you absorb some of that thing's memories.

I guess that really is a lot like a video game.

When I looked more closely at my card, I found the words SKILL POINTS, along with the number 3. I could use those points to gain some abilities.

"Now, then. We're buying two Giant Toads from you; along with the quest completion award, that comes to 110,000 eris."

110,000.

Minus the cost of transport, each of those frogs was worth five thousand yen. The reward for actually completing the quest was another hundred thousand.

According to Aqua, most parties had four to six people when they attempted a quest. So think of an average party of adventurers risking their lives in pitched battle for a day or two and coming home with five frog carcasses. Along with the completion award, they would make 125,000 yen. In a five-person party, each party member would come away with 25,000 yen.

…That was so not worth it.

You'd be talking about a rate of 25,000 yen a day, *if* the quest took only one day. That might sound like a pretty good deal to the average person, but remember we were putting our lives on the line here. If even one more toad had popped up today, for example, I might've been eaten, too, and there would've been no one to help us. Party wipe. The hairs on the back of my neck stood up just thinking about it.

I took a look at the other quests on the board:

Cut down Egil Trees causing trouble in the woods. Reward by volume.

Please help me find my lost pet, White Wolf!

Seeking swordsmanship tutor for my son. Note: only Rune Knights or Sword Masters need apply.

Do YOU want to be part of my magical experiments? Note: must have exceptional HP or strong Magic Defense.

Phew.

This world sure didn't make it easy for you.

I'd been an adventurer for only two days, and I already wanted to return to Japan.

"Pardon me, may I have a moment…?"

I was sitting in a chair nearby, nursing a bout of homesickness, when a soft voice came from behind me. I looked up with eyes deadened by the realities of this fantasy world.

"Sure… How can I help…y…?"

And then I saw the owner of the voice and was at a loss for words.

A female Knight.

And a drop-dead gorgeous one, at that.

She was looking at me expressionlessly; she gave off an almost palpable cool.

She was just a little bit taller than I am. (I'm five foot four, so she was maybe, say, five six?) She wore sturdy-looking metal armor, and golden hair framed her blue eyes. I guessed she was a year or two older than me.

Her armor hid just what type of body she had, but something about her was incredibly sexy. Despite her cool look, she gave off the impression of…suffering, somehow.

Whoa, hang on! I can't go falling in love at first sight!

"Uh, yes, um…what can I do for you?" I could deal with someone younger than me, like Megumin, or someone who was (or at least looked) my age, like Aqua, but my voice cracked a little with nervousness as I talked to this obviously older woman.

That's what I get for being a lifelong *hikikomori*.

"Tell me, was it your party that posted this for recruitment? Are you by any chance still recruiting?"

The female Knight held out a piece of paper. I'd forgotten we hadn't taken down the recruitment notice since adding Megumin.

"Oh, that. Yes, we're still looking for more members, but to be perfectly honest, I can't recommend it—"

"Please! Oh, please let me be in your party!"

I'd been trying to put her off gently, but the Knight suddenly grabbed my hand.

…Huh?

"Wh-wh-wh-whoa, hold on. I should warn you—we have a lot of problems. Neither of the other members is even slightly capable, and I'm in the lowest class! In fact, just a little while ago, both my friends wound up covered in slime— Ow ow ow ow!"

She'd squeezed my hand extra hard the moment I said "covered in slime."

"I knew those were your companions I saw earlier with all that goop on them! How did they end up like that? Please let me get...get covered in..."

"What?!"

What did she just say?

"W-wait, let me try again! What I mean is, how could I, a Knight, overlook two tender young women in such a state? How about it? I'm a Crusader, an advanced class of Knight. I believe that fits your requirements."

What was with this girl? She was giving me the crazy eye. She'd seemed so calm just a moment ago!

A red flag went up in my mind. This girl had *something* in common with Aqua and Megumin.

I hated to turn down a looker, but I had no choice.

"Wellll, I'm sorry, but as I said a moment ago, I really can't recommend this party. One of our members has yet to be of any use to anybody, and the other can cast only a single spell per day. And, again, I'm the lowest possible class. We're one dysfunctional group, so I really recommend you look elsewh—!"

Her grip on my hand tightened further.

"That's even better! The truth is... It's hard to say out loud, but I'm really... I'm confident in my defensive abilities—I am! But I'm a bit of a klutz, and my...my attacks never hit, so..."

Good old reliable intuition.

"So I'm an advanced class, but it's not a big deal! I want you to send me right out front—use me as a shield!"

The female Knight brought her face, with its graceful features, close to mine as I sat in my chair.

Very…very…close…

Because I was seated, she stood above me, but she'd gotten so near that her long golden hair brushed my cheeks and set my heart pounding.

Now I was *really* paying for that *hikikomori* life…!

No! No, I wasn't. This was just too much stimulation for an adolescent virgin, and it was throwing me off. *Stay calm! Don't get taken in by her wiles!*

"Now, now, how could we use a woman as a shield? We really are an extremely weak party, ma'am, so I think you'd wind up as a monster's punching bag on every single quest."

"That's what I'm looking for."

"N-no, it's not! Just today, my two companions were eaten by Giant Toads and ended up all slimy! Seriously, that's likely to happen every single day…!"

"That's exactly what I'm looking for!"

…Now I get it.

The female Knight gripping my hand and blushing? As I looked at her, it finally dawned on me. It wasn't just her abilities that wouldn't help us. Like the rest of my party, she was useless to the core.

Chapter 2

May There Be Treasure (By Which I Mean Panties) in This Right Hand!

1

"Hey, I've been meaning to ask… How exactly do you acquire skills?"

It was the day after we'd fought the Giant Toads. We were having a late lunch at the Guild tavern. In front of me, Megumin, who apparently had no money and had been unable to eat anything decent until she met us, was single-mindedly working her way through a combo meal. Aqua was getting a nearby waiter to bring her seconds.

She sure had a fine appetite for a woman her age.

You'd think a party of two girls and one guy would basically be a starter harem, but this wasn't hot at all.

Megumin looked up, fork still in hand.

"How to learn skills? Why, from the place on your card that shows currently available skills, of course… Oh, your class is Adventurer, is it not? Since that's a starter class, you have to have someone teach you new skills. Have them show you a skill, then guide you through it. Then it will appear on your card, and you can allocate points to it. Simple."

Okay.

I was pretty sure the clerk at the Guild said Adventurers could learn any skill. Meaning…

"Meaning if I got you to show me how to do it, Megumin, I could even learn Explosion?"

"Yes, exactly!"

"Wow!"

She became inordinately excited by my offhanded question.

"Yes, that is it exactly, Kazuma! It would take an outrageous number of points, true, but Adventurer is the only other class beside Arch-wizard that can learn Explosion. If you'd like to learn it, I will show it to you as many times as you want! After all, is there any other skill that is even worth learning? No, of course not! Now, Kazuma, join me on the explosive path!"

Her face was so very…very…close…

"C-calm down already, jailbait! I only have three skill points, anyway. Can I learn Explosion with that?"

"J-jailbait…?!"

Megumin was too overcome to continue the conversation, so I turned to Aqua.

"An Adventurer who wanted to learn Explosion wouldn't manage it with ten or twenty points," she said. "If you worked at it for about ten years, saving up every single skill point, you *might* be able to learn it."

"Who would wait that long?"

"Y-you say I…am jailbait…?"

Megumin, seemingly in a state of shock at my turn of phrase, hung her head and returned to wolfing down her meal.

Anyway, since the ability to learn any skill at all was one of the few advantages of my class, I might as well make the most of it.

"Hey, Aqua. You must know all kinds of useful skills, right? Teach me something easy. Something that won't take too many points but will still be helpful. I'm looking for a good deal here."

Aqua held her water glass thoughtfully and was quiet for a moment.

"…Wellll, all right. But just so you know, my skills are serious stuff. I don't go around teaching them to just anybody, got it?"

There was Aqua, trying to make herself look important again—but since I needed her to teach me, I would just have to tolerate it.

Nodding solemnly, I watched Aqua perform her skill.

"First, look at this glass. It's full of water, right? You're going to take it and balance it on top of your head so it doesn't fall off. Here, try it."

I managed to steady the glass on top of my head, all too aware of the stares of bystanders.

Then Aqua produced a seed of some kind from who knew where and set it on top of the table.

"Now use your finger to flick the seed up into the glass. If you get it, presto! The seed will absorb the water in the glass, and—"

"Hey, who asked to learn party tricks, you useless goddess?!"

"Whaaaat?!"

She seemed excessively surprised by my reaction and joined Megumin in sitting dejectedly. She idly flicked the seed around the table.

I didn't know what she was so upset about, but I wished she would take that stupid glass off her head. It was attracting attention.

Suddenly, someone nearby piped up:

"Ha-ha-ha! You're a funny one! Hey, are you that party Darkness wants to get in on? You want to learn something useful? How about some Thief skills?"

That's when I saw the two women at the next table over. The one who'd called out was a youngish girl with silver hair, very attractive, wearing leather armor and a casual air. There was a small cut on her cheek. She seemed a bit cunning, but also open and cheerful.

Beside her sat a lovely girl with long golden hair and a full set of plate mail. She seemed cool and aloof and…

Wait. Wasn't she the female Knight who'd tried to join the party the day before?

The "Thief" looked to be a year or two younger than me.

"Um, Thief skills? What kind of skills are those?"

The girl seemed pleased by my question. "I'm glad you asked. They're *very* useful, for starters. You can detect and disarm traps; you can set an ambush or steal an item. There are even a bunch of great passive abilities. Your class is Adventurer, right? Well, you don't even need many points to learn Thief skills. It's a great deal. What do you say? I'll teach you some for the price of one Crimson Beer!"

So cheap!

And on reflection, I realized there was no risk in having this girl teach me something. If I wanted to learn more Thief skills, I could always ask any of the Thieves wandering around town.

"All right—it's a deal! Waiter! One Crimson Beer for the lady, please!"

2

"Maybe I should start by introducing myself. I'm Chris. I'm a Thief, as you can see. And this boor here is Darkness. I think you've already met. She's a Crusader, so I don't know if she'll have that many skills you'd want to learn."

"Great! My name's Kazuma. Nice to meet you, Chris!"

The three of us were all but alone in the square behind the Adventurers Guild.

I'd left the other two to mope back at our table.

"All right, maybe we should start with Sense Foe and Ambush. We'll have to take a rain check on Disarm Trap, since there aren't many traps around town. Let's see... Darkness, turn around for a second, would you?"

"Huh? All right..."

She turned her back as she'd been told.

Chris hopped into a barrel a short distance away so that only her upper body was visible. Then she pitched a stone at Darkness's head and ducked down into the barrel.

...Was that supposed to be the ambush?

Without a word, Darkness strode toward the only barrel in sight.

"*Sense Foe... Sense Foe...* I can sense Darkness's rage approaching!

Hey, Darkness? You know I'm only doing this to teach the guy some skills, right? Right?! Be gentl—aahhhh, stoppitttt!" Chris shouted as Darkness turned the barrel on its side and sent it rolling away.

Can I really learn anything this way...?

"O-okay, then. How about you try my number one recommendation, Steal? It snags a single item from the target. Doesn't matter if it's a sword they're clutching or a purse buried deep in their pack. One random item. The success rate depends on your Luck stat. It can do some pretty great stuff. Maybe you're facing down a fearsome enemy, and you grab his weapon or you nab some hidden treasure he's got and then make a break for it."

Chris had collected her wits after her ride in the barrel, and she was filling me in on the finer points of the Steal skill. It certainly did sound useful. And if it was really based on your Luck, I finally had a chance to make use of my one good stat.

"I'm gonna use it on you now, okay?" Chris said. "Ready?" She held out her hand, shouted "*Steal!*" and suddenly, she was holding a small object.

It was...

"My wallet! Hey!"

Not that there was much in it.

"Ooh, score! That's how you use Steal. Here's your wal—" Chris stopped as she was about to hand the wallet back to me, and a smile crept over her face. "Hey," she said, "how about a little contest? Learn Steal right now. Then, steal any one item from me. My purse, my weapon—it's all fair game. Whatever you get, it's got to be worth more than this ratty thing." She gave my wallet a shake. "So I'll keep this wallet, and whatever you get from me, you keep it in exchange. What do you think? Wanna give it a try?"

She sure came up with some strange ideas.

But I stopped and thought about it. I had high Luck. And I could steal any one thing from her...

In other words, even if the skill failed, I probably wouldn't walk away empty-handed.

Why not give it a try? A bet like this seemed like the sort of thing only a couple of crazy adventurers could get up to, anyway—I loved it!

For the first time since I got to this world, I'd found something that made me feel like a real adventurer!

When I checked my Adventurer's Card, I found a new field, AVAILABLE SKILLS. When I touched it with my finger, four skills appeared:

SENSE FOE... 1 POINT

AMBUSH... 1 POINT

STEAL... 1 POINT

THE WONDERS OF NATURE... 5 POINTS

The Wonders of Nature? Was that the seed-in-a-glass party trick Aqua had shown me? That was some name for a parlor trick! ...Huh? *It took more skill points than everything else combined!*

I admit I was intrigued by the party trick, but I took in the other skills on my card—Sense Foe, Ambush, and Steal. That used up my three skill points, so the AVAILABLE POINTS field now showed zero.

So this was how you learned skills around here.

"All right, I've learned it. And you're on! No matter what I steal—no complaining, right?" I stuck out my right hand. Strangely, Chris was smiling.

"Good! I like a man who doesn't back down from a challenge! I wonder what you'll get? You might just recover your wallet. First prize is this enchanted dagger—it won't sell for less than 400,000 eris. And I even have a consolation prize—these rocks I picked up earlier to throw at Darkness!"

"Hey! That's a dirty trick!" I said, looking at the collection of pebbles in Chris's hand.

I *wondered* why she seemed so confident!

I guess carrying around a bunch of junk items was one way to thwart Steal.

"Call it your tuition fee. No skill is all-powerful. With a little imagination, you can come up with a counter to anything. Lesson learned? Now, go for it!"

Dammit. Lesson learned, all right. Seeing Chris grin at me, I even felt like a bit of an idiot for letting her game me like that.

This wasn't Japan. This was a world of survival of the fittest. It was my own fault for being gullible.

Anyway, my odds might have been lower, but the contest wasn't over yet.

"All right, here I come! Luck's always been the only thing I've ever had on my side... *Steal*!"

As I shouted, I found myself grasping something tightly in my outstretched right hand.

First try! Good luck really was my one gift.

I opened my hand and took a close look at what I'd snatched...

"...The heck is this?"

It was a single piece of white cloth. I held it up to the light...

"Yahoooo! This is even better than first prize!"

"Awww, nooo! Gimme back my pantiiiieeeees!" Chris shouted tearfully, holding down her skirt.

3

When I got back to the Guild tavern after learning my new skills, I found it in an uproar.

"Milady Aqua, do it again! I'll pay! Show us The Wonders of Nature again!"

"You idiot! Our dear Aqua doesn't want money—she wants food! Right, my dear?! I'll treat you! So show us The Wonders of Nature again!"

For some reason, a crowd surrounded Aqua. She looked more than a little annoyed.

"This is art! It's not something you can do just any old time someone asks! A great man once said, a good joke is only good once. I'm not some third-rate street player who'll do the same thing over and over just because it's a little popular! In fact, I'm not a performer at all, so I'm hardly interested in making money from my art! That's the very least someone can commit to when they seek to refine their skills. Anyway, The Wonders of Nature was never something I intended to show to you lot, and— Hey, Kazuma! You're finally back. Y'know, it's your fault this is happen— Say, what's with her?"

Aqua had noticed the wet-eyed, sulky Chris who accompanied me as I pushed my way through the crowd.

Darkness opened her mouth before I could explain. "Chris is upset because not only did Kazuma take her panties, but then he held them for ransom."

"Hey, way to run your mouth! Hold on! Wait! I mean—she's not wrong, but—really, wait!"

Chris had wept that she would pay anything I asked if I would let her have her panties back, so I'd told her she should set the price for her own intimates. That was all.

And then I'd added that if I didn't like the price she named, I would just keep the panties and take them back to become an heirloom of my house.

She'd pulled out her wallet, along with the one she'd taken from me, and traded them for the underwear. Darkness made it sound so *unseemly*.

I was starting to squirm under Aqua's and Megumin's gazes, taken in as they were by Darkness's telling, but then Chris raised her dejected face.

"Well, I guess getting your underwear snatched in public is no reason to get in a mood! All right, Darkness. Sorry, but I'm gonna hit up a well-stocked dungeon I know and do some grinding. I did just use up all my money to get back my hostage panties."

"Hey, hang on! Aqua and Megumin I'm used to, but every female adventurer in the room is glaring at me now! Just wait!"

It looked like most of the women there had overheard our conversation. Chris snickered at my anxious expression and said, "Just a little revenge, eh? All right, I'm off to make some cash, so play nice, Darkness! Catch you all later!"

With that, Chris made for the adventurer recruitment board.

"Um…aren't you going with her, Miss, uh, Darkness?" I asked. The Knight still sat at our table like it was the most natural thing in the world.

"No… I'm a frontline defender. We're an eris a dozen. Thieves, though—you can't tackle a dungeon without one, but it's not a flashy job, so there aren't many. Everyone wants someone like Chris."

I see. Come to think of it, Aqua said Arch-priests were in high demand, too. I guess your occupation could get you more than I'd realized.

A few minutes later, we saw Chris walk out the door of the Guild with several other adventurers in a party she'd found. She gave us a jaunty wave as she left.

"They're going to a dungeon now, even though it's almost dark?"

"First thing in the morning is the best time to tackle a dungeon," Megumin said. "So it is quite common for people to go to a dungeon the night before and camp out at the entrance. There are even some merchants who set up shop outside dungeons specifically to cater to adventurers who are camped there. So, how did it go, Kazuma? Did you learn a new skill?"

A shameless smile grew on my face at hearing Megumin's question.

"Heh-heh, how about I show you? Here I go—*Steal*!" I shouted, and thrust my right hand toward Megumin. In a flash, I was holding a piece of white cloth.

Yup. Panties again.

"I do not understand. Did your stats go up enough for you to change jobs from Adventurer to Pervert?" She paused. "Um…it's rather chilly, so could you please return my panties…?"

"Wh-what? That's weird… It's not… I mean, it's supposed to take something random!"

I hurriedly returned the panties to Megumin, and as the looks of the women nearby went from chilly to freezing, I heard someone pound the table with a slam.

It was Darkness, rising from her chair. For some reason, her eyes were ablaze…

"I knew it! I knew I had judged correctly! You beast—stealing the panties of such a young girl right out in public! I absolutely—I absolutely must be part of this party!"

"Nope."

"Wh…a…?! Hrrk…!" At my answer, Darkness turned red and began to shake.

What was I supposed to do? I wasn't sure how, but I could tell this female Knight was not the useful type.

So of course, Aqua and Megumin were immediately interested in her.

"Hey, Kazuma, who's this? Is this that girl you said you interviewed while Megumin and I were at the bathhouse yesterday?"

"Wait, is she not a Crusader? Why should you wish to refuse such a powerful ally?"

With one eye on Darkness, they each offered their altogether unsolicited opinions.

Dammit… And here I'd worked so hard to put her off yesterday… I *so* didn't want her to meet these two.

All right, let's try this:

"Listen, Darkness. Aqua and I may not look like much, but we have a job to do. We need to defeat the Demon King." Aqua, of course, wanted to get back to the divine realm, but for my part—having been confronted by the reality of a world in which we could barely handle an overgrown frog, let alone a demonic sovereign—I was no longer feeling very enthusiastic about that task.

I paid no attention to Megumin, who sat next to us pretending to studiously ignore our conversation.

Wait. Actually, this might be the perfect moment.

"This goes for you, too, Megumin," I said. "Aqua and I want to defeat the Demon King at any cost. That's why we became adventurers. And because of that, things are likely to get pretty rough for us. Especially for you, Darkness—you're a lady Knight! Do you know what the Demon King would do to you if he captured you?"

"I know exactly what you're talking about!" Darkness said. "From time immemorial it has been the role of the lady Knight to be the erotic plaything of the Demon King! Just that alone is enough to make me join you!"

"Huh? Say what?!" Her eagerness brought me up short.

"Huh? What about what? Did I say something strange?"

All right, let's leave that one for now. I turned to Megumin.

"Megumin, look—we're up against the Demon King here. Aqua and I are taking the fight to the most powerful creature in this world. You don't have to force yourself to stick with such a crazy bunch of—"

Bam.

Megumin suddenly stood up. Her mantle fluttered out.

"My name is Megumin! First among the spell-casters of the Crimson Magic Clan and wielder of Explosion! Is the Demon King known as the strongest in this world? Then I shall topple him with the strongest magic in this world!"

We were getting odd looks from around the hall as Megumin made her proud, and thoroughly tweeny, declaration.

Useless. Don't give me that self-satisfied smirk, you!

What was I gonna do? The two problem children I most wanted out of my party were the ones most eager to be in it!

"Hey, Kazuma! Kazumaaa!" As I sat there stewing, Aqua tugged on my sleeve. "After hearing all that stuff you were just saying? I'm not so sure about this anymore… Isn't there an easier way to beat the Demon King?"

...You better get on board. Aren't you the one who needs to defeat him most of all?

At that moment...

"*Urgent quest! Urgent quest!* All adventurers currently in town, please report immediately to the Guild Hall. Repeat, all adventurers, please report immediately to the Guild Hall!"

The announcement boomed through the streets. Maybe they were amplifying it with magic?

"Hey, what do they mean, an urgent quest? Is a monster attacking the town or something?" I was pretty concerned. Darkness and Megumin, on the other hand, looked thrilled.

"Hmm, it's probably about the cabbage harvest," Darkness said happily. "It's almost the season."

I was silent for a long moment.

"Huh? *Cabbage?* Is that the name of a monster?" I said dumbly. Megumin and Darkness both gave me a strange look of pity.

"Cabbages are green and round," Megumin said. "You eat them."

"They're a crunchy, delicious vegetable," Darkness added.

"I know what a cabbage is! So, what? They're putting out an urgent quest so we can all go and do farmwork?"

Granted, I'd been in construction myself until just a little while ago, but I didn't come here for agriculture.

"Oh... Kazuma, I guess you might not know, but...the cabbages around here—" Aqua was hesitantly trying to tell me something, but the desk clerk cut her off with a loud announcement to the adventurers in the hall.

"Everyone, please pardon our sudden call! Some of you have figured this out already, but it's cabbage season! The time for this year's harvest has come! The cabbages are quite full this year, so we will be paying ten thousand eris a head! We have already instructed the townspeople to evacuate their homes. Please catch as many cabbages as you're able and bring them back here. Please take care so their counterattacks don't hurt you! Finally, because of the large number of people involved, we will pay out the reward at a later date."

…Wait, what did she just say?!

A cheer went up outside the Guild Hall.

I followed the crowd to see what was going on and saw a bunch of round green objects floating nonchalantly around the streets.

As I stood there trying to take it in, Aqua appeared beside me and said solemnly, "The cabbages here can fly. They get more flavorful as the harvest approaches, but they don't have any intention of ending up on the menu without a fight. They make a run for it through the towns and fields and head out to sea. It's said they cross the ocean and spend their days quietly in a place no one knows, where they can live out their lives without being eaten. But if we can catch even one, we'll get an awfully good meal out of it."

"I wonder if I could just go back to the stable and hit the hay…," I muttered dimly. Next to me, a couple of adventurers braver than I were joining the chase with a shout. Their manly fervor seemed to be stoked by the cabbages' own desire to survive.

As the adventurers threw themselves into combat with the vegetables, I had only one thought in mind.

How sad is it that I have to fight to the death with some leafy greens?
I wanna go back to Japan…

4

I tried a bite of the stir-fried cabbage they were serving up at the Guild.

"I don't get it. How in the world can a regular cabbage stir-fry be this good? It makes no sense!"

The harvest was safely over, and all around town, people were trying out different recipes using the stuff.

In the end, I'd forced myself to be part of the cabbage hunt because the money was good, but I felt a twinge of regret. I didn't come all the way to a fantasy world to fight with a bunch of vegetables.

"Way to go, Darkness!" Aqua was saying. "You really are a Crusader. Those vegetables didn't stand a chance against your iron defense!"

"Oh, no," Darkness replied, "I'm just tough. I'm clumsy and not very quick, so I can hardly hit anything with a sword. Acting as a human wall to protect my party is my only real talent." She paused. "That's why Megumin impressed me so much. She's the one who brought down in one magnificent explosion all those monsters who'd followed the cabbages into town. You sure took all the adventurers there by surprise!"

"Heh-heh-heh. None can stand against my Explosion spell." Megumin took a breath. "Really, though, Kazuma was remarkable. After I'd collapsed from my spell, he rushed out, collected me, and brought me back."

"True," Darkness said. "When I was surrounded by monsters and cabbages all making me their punching bag, it was Kazuma who appeared and harvested the vegetables. You saved me, Kazuma. I thank you."

"I saw him hide with his Ambush skill, track their movements with Sense Foe, and finally hit them from behind with a powerful Steal attack," Megumin said. "It was like watching a master assassin at work."

Finally, there was a *clink* as Aqua set down a plateful of the conquered cabbage. The useless goddess had spent the entire harvest running this way and that by herself, just going after whatever cabbage was nearest, accomplishing nothing. Now she wiped her lips daintily.

"Kazuma... By my name, I hereby give you the title 'Beautiful Cabbage Thief.'"

"That's ridiculous! If anyone ever calls me that, I'll pop 'em right in the mouth! Arrrrgh, how did things come to this...?" I leaned on the table with my head in my hands.

This was an emergency.

"Anyway… My name is Darkness. My class is Crusader. I carry a two-handed sword, but please do not expect too much from me in battle. I'm so clumsy my attacks rarely land. But I'm very good at being a human shield. I look forward to adventuring with you all!"

That's right…I had another new party member.

Aqua, looking quite pleased, said, "Hee-hee! Our group is starting to look pretty impressive, huh? There's me, the Arch-priest. Megumin, the Arch-wizard. And Darkness, a Crusader who specializes in frontline defense. How many parties are there where three out of the four members are from advanced classes, huh, Kazuma? You are so lucky! You ought to be grateful!"

Sure, lucky. I've got a spell-caster who can use only one spell per day, a frontline fighter whose attacks never hit, and the world's dumbest, unluckiest Arch-priest, who—by the way—*still hasn't done a single useful thing*!

Aqua and Megumin had really hit it off with Darkness during the cabbage hunt, and all of a sudden they'd invited her to be in our party.

Normally, I'd have no reason to refuse. I mean, she was gorgeous.

But Darkness—when she said her attacks never land, she meant it. Like, *never*.

She really is gorgeous, though.

Because she put every one of her skill points into defensive abilities, she'd never learned things like Two-Handed Sword—in other words, the offensive skills that give you basic competency in the use of a weapon.

What a waste for a girl who was so cool and so hot at the same time.

This Crusader of ours also had a weird habit of jumping right into the middle of a horde of monsters. I appreciated that a Crusader, whose whole duty was to protect the weak, would want more than anyone to leap into the fray and help others, but…

"Ergh… Ohh… When those cabbages and monsters were beating me up, I could hardly *stand* it… It looks like I'm the only frontline defense this party has, so don't hesitate to offer me up as a hostage or use me as a human shield. If you decide you must sacrifice me to an awful fate to save yourselves from danger, please feel free to do so… Mm! J-just imagining it has me shaking…with excitement…"

Her cheeks had turned a pale red, and she was shivering a little.

Wait—I get it.

She's just a garden-variety masochist.

Now when I looked at her, I didn't see a hot girl—just a sexual deviant.

"So, Kazuma. I might—no, I'm sure I will—be an albatross around this party's neck at times, so when I am, please, please punish me mercilessly for it. I look forward to working with you!"

An Arch-priest who knew every healing spell. An Arch-wizard who could use the world's strongest magic. And a Crusader with an impenetrable defense.

It sounded perfect on paper. And yet right now, the only feeling I had about the future was a bad one.

5

My adventurer level rose to 6.

In other words, I went up two levels after the cabbage hunt.

I hadn't even defeated them—just captured them. So why did my level go up?

For that matter, why in the world were cabbages worth so much XP?

There were so many questions. But thinking about them made my head hurt, so I decided to just let them go.

You couldn't let the ifs and ands of this world overwhelm you.

Cabbages were worth ten thousand eris a head. This was apparently because you could gain XP by eating them fresh. Meaning, adventurers with enough cash could grow stronger by just having a meal.

With my new levels came more skill points.

Trying to figure out why you got skill points when you leveled—something ripped straight out of a role-playing game—would probably have me losing sleep over it, so I didn't bother.

Like I said, you just couldn't let it get to you.

When I'd leveled up, I'd received two skill points.

A magic-user and a warrior from another party I met during the cabbage hunt had taught me One-Handed Sword and Basic Magic. Each cost me one point.

The One-Handed Sword skill, obviously, allowed you to ably wield a one-handed sword. With that, I gained an average ability to use a weapon.

I was now out of skill points again, but I wanted to learn magic even more than how to use a sword. Who could possibly come to a world that had magic and not want to try it out?

Basic Magic allowed you to use simple spells related to the four elements—fire, water, earth, and air. Incidentally, these basics weren't powerful enough to kill or even hurt anything; most casters skipped Basic Magic entirely, saved up their points, and jumped right to mid-level magic.

Intermediate Magic cost ten skill points. My Magic stat wasn't very high, so at that price maybe I should just give up on learning offensive spells.

I'd heard some people began with a certain number of skill points based on natural talent. These prodigies weren't as rare as you'd think, and they could start out with ten or even twenty points, taking an advanced class immediately.

Megumin and Darkness, for example, must have been pretty well received when they started out. (Aqua didn't count.)

While I, at level 1, had zero skill points.

...Not gonna think about it too hard. I'll just get depressed.

The more skills I learned, the more like a real adventurer I became.

All that was left was the outfit.

Sometimes I changed into clothes that I'd bought in this world, but for the most part it was just me, my tracksuit, and a short sword. I really needed some armor. Even just a bit of leather.

And so...

"Why do I have to come along on your dumb shopping trip?"

Aqua complained loudly as we walked into the armor shop.

"Because you need some equipment, too. I may be wearing a tracksuit, but what have you got? A flimsy little feather mantle?" Aqua, like me, was still wearing the same thing she'd had on when we got to this world.

Every night after changing into her pajamas, she washed it in a bucket from the inn—*splash, splash, splash*—then put it out to dry in the same place where they dried the horses' hay.

"Dummy," Aqua said, looking put out. "You seem to be forgetting that I'm a goddess. This feather mantle is holy. It's a unique item imbued with all kinds of magical properties—status conditions don't affect it, and it's got exceptional durability. Lots of good stuff. There's no equipment better!"

I considered suggesting she not hang her holy, divine super-item out with the horse feed.

"Hey, sounds good. If we're ever strapped for cash, we can sell that thing... Ooh, this chest plate is made of leather, but it looks like a good start."

"H-hey, you were just joking, right? This cloak is pretty much the only proof that I'm a goddess. You'd never really sell it, right? Right...?"

6

"Oh-ho. It seems clothes really do make the man!"

"Indeed. Kazuma at last looks the part of an adventurer."

In the Guild Hall, which had become our unofficial meeting spot, Darkness and Megumin admired my new outfit.

I sort of wanted to ask what exactly they thought I'd looked like before. Just some creeper?

Now I looked like I belonged here. I had a leather chest plate, metal gauntlets, and metal greaves.

Aqua had said that my tracksuit alone killed the immersion around here, so the day before, I'd bought several sets of appropriate clothes.

I'd been told that magical skills usually required a free hand, and since I had gone out of my way to learn some magic, I decided not to carry a shield. I had just the blade at my hip, in a style I liked to think of as a sort of magical swordsman.

I'd used up most of the money I'd made off my little Steal contest with Chris, but there was enough left over from that to put food on the table for another week or two.

And, hey—I had some armor; I'd learned some skills. I wanted to go on a quest.

When I told everyone about it, Darkness firmly nodded.

"It's mating season for the Giant Toads, and many of them are near town. We could—"

"No more toads!" Megumin and Aqua interrupted in unison.

"...Why not? They're easy to stab with a bladed weapon, which makes them easy to kill. Their only attack is to try to grab you with their tongue. You can sell the carcass as a consumable, so you can make good money on them. You might get eaten if you're wearing only thin armor, but they hate metal, so I assume Kazuma wouldn't be targeted the way he's dressed now. As for you two, Aqua and Megumin, I'll act as a shield for you."

"Oh... These two were traumatized when toads ate them a while ago. They wound up covered in slime from head to toe. It's all right; let's find something else."

For some reason, Darkness's cheeks had gone a light red at my words.

"...Don't tell me that thought excites you."

"It does not."

She looked away bashfully, but I had a bad feeling. She wasn't going to disappear on a one-woman frog chase the minute I took my eyes off her, was she?

"Not counting that urgent cabbage hunt," I said, "this will be the first quest for the four of us together. It'd be nice if we could just take it easy."

Megumin and Darkness went over to the board to see if there were any simple quests posted.

Aqua rolled her eyes at me and said, "What can you expect from a hikiNEET introvert? Kazuma, you're in the weakest class, so I can see why you'd want to be cautious, but think about the rest of us. You've got a party full of advanced adventurers! Why not take on some tougher quests, make some real money, raise our levels—and then it's 'Good-bye, Demon King!' What I mean is, let's pick the most difficult mission we can find!"

I was silent for a long moment. Then I said, "I hate to tell you this, but...you have yet to be any help at all." Aqua seemed aghast at my words, but I paid her no mind. I went on. "I'm pretty sure I was supposed to get some superpowerful item or ability from you so I wouldn't have any trouble here. And look, I'm the last person to complain when the gods themselves give me free swag. But didn't I pick you over all the other stuff I could've had? And now that we've come this far, I have to ask: Have you done anything for me—*anything*—that's better than whatever legendary loot or killer special ability I would've gotten? How about it? Back when we got here, you were sure you were all that, but you still haven't proved it, you self-proclaimed *former* you-know-what!"

"*Sniff...* I-I'm not a *former*... I-I'm still...still a goddess," Aqua said despondently.

I practically shouted now. "'Goddess'! You?! A goddess would give guidance to her hero! She'd fight the Demon King herself, seal him away until the hero was ready! And what did *you* do on our cabbage hunt? Sure, you somehow wound up with a bunch of them, but all I saw was you crying while flying vegetables chased you around! What kind of deity gets bullied by something that goes in stew? The only thing you know how to do is get eaten by frogs; your only abilities are stupid party tricks—and you call yourself a goddess?!"

"W-*waaaaahh!*"

I felt a bit satisfied seeing Aqua collapsed over the table, weeping. I'd gotten my revenge on her for making fun of me.

But Aqua, it seemed, wasn't ready to let it drop. She looked up from the table and said, "I—I can do lots of useful things! I know healing magic, and…healing magic, and—healing magic! So what about it, you hikiNEET? How long do you think it'll take to defeat the Demon King at this rate, huh? If you've got ideas, I'd love to hear them!" *She thinks she's clever.*

Aqua glared at me through teary eyes.

I sneered at her. "I cut class every day of high school to stay home and work on my pro gaming career. You really think I don't have any idea how to handle this?"

"You were a pro gamer?"

"No, I just wanted to say it. Listen, Aqua. I don't have amazing powers like the usual protagonists of these stories. But I do have the things I learned in Japan. So I was thinking, what if I made simple Japanese goods, something traditional they don't have here, and sell them? I've got good Luck, right? Even the girl who registered us said I should go into trading. It got me thinking, maybe adventuring isn't the only way to make money around here. We can take other routes, too. As long as we've got some cash, it won't be hard to get XP. We can buy cabbage, or whatever else gives you XP just by eating it, and get stronger *that* way."

True, the other Japanese here knew the same things I did. But unlike me, they'd taken the special powers as they were supposed to. They wouldn't think to do something so menial as selling handmade goods—they'd be too focused on their quests.

Basically, the ROI from adventuring for me wasn't very good.

I'd only been on a frog hunt and cabbage hunt so far, but looking at the quest board, nothing seemed to offer a reward proportionate to its dangers.

Life was just too cheap here.

Sure, I periodically brought up the Demon King in front of Aqua for her benefit, but to tell you the truth, I wasn't thinking seriously about defeating him. Which meant instead, I had to figure out how to live in this world with the least fuss and the most comfort.

"A-anyway, you get thinking, too! Think of something easy we can sell! And teach me that recovery magic of yours already! I want to be able to heal when I have enough skill points!"

"Nooo! Not my healing magic! I'll lose my reason for existing! You don't need to learn those spells! You have me! Nooo!" She flopped on the table and began weeping about me taking away the one thing that gave her existence any value.

That was how Megumin and Darkness found us when they came back.

"What have you been up to?" Megumin asked. "You can be rather cruel, Kazuma. You could probably make any girl cry if you told her how you really feel."

"Hmm…," Darkness said. "If you need to let off some stress, why not leave Aqua alone and insult me instead?" She paused. "After all, it is a Crusader's duty to stand in harm's way for others."

Both of them looked at Aqua, who was still crying. She seemed to realize everyone was staring at her and buried her face in her arms, peering out periodically from between her limbs to glare at me. It was kind of annoying.

"Look, just ignore her. But Darkness…" I glanced at her. "I didn't know you were so svelte under all that armor." Darkness was wearing only a black tank top, a tight black skirt, and leather boots. She still wore the great sword across her back, making her look less like a Knight than a simple warrior.

Apparently her armor was in the shop, having been damaged when she took that beating from the cabbages. I found myself unexpectedly speaking more gently to the unprotected Darkness.

She was firm where a woman ought to be firm and had a very shapely form. Frankly, she was turning me on.

Standing next to Megumin only highlighted how developed Darkness was. I started to think that for a face that lovely and a body so smoking, I could maybe overlook some personal quirks…

"Oh!" she cried out. "Did you just say, 'How dare this pig have such a hot body'?"

"No! I didn't!"

I glanced at Megumin and Aqua…

You know what? I take it back. It doesn't matter how hot she is. Personality trumps all.

Then Megumin exclaimed, "Hey! Explain the meaning of that glance you just gave me!"

"There's no meaning. I was just thinking, 'Thank god I'm not into jailbait,' is all."

"Start a fight with someone of the Crimson Magic Clan, and she will always finish it!" Megumin said, tugging on my sleeve. "Let us step outside and—"

"Um, anyway…," Darkness broke in. "If we're going to do a quest, how about one that will help Aqua gain some levels?"

"What do you mean?" I said. "Is anyone offering one that convenient?" And Aqua had learned pretty much every skill there was for her to learn with her starting points, anyway, so I didn't think she needed to be too worried about leveling up.

"As a rule, it's hard for Priests to level up, since they lack real offensive capabilities. They can't run out and just kill something like a warrior can or rush in with a blast of magic like a Wizard. So Priests prefer to hunt the undead. They're immortal monsters that have turned against the laws of the gods. The power of the divine has an opposite effect on the undead. Hit them with healing magic, and it actually destroys them."

Now that I thought about it, that sounded familiar. It was pretty similar in most video games: Recovery magic works as an attack against undead enemies.

I dunno, though. Would a few levels even help this useless goddess?

Then I had a flash of inspiration.

When my level went up, so did my stats. Would it be the same for Aqua?

She was still slumped over the table, crying crocodile tears and peeking at us every once in a while to see if we were paying attention. If this idiot's level went up, would her Intelligence stat rise a little bit, too? That would be the most efficient way to make her more useful in battle.

"Hey, that's not a bad idea," I said. "But Darkness, your armor isn't back from the shop yet…"

Darkness crossed her arms and proclaimed, "Ahem! Not a problem for me! I didn't specialize in defensive skills for nothing. Even without armor, I'm tougher than an Adamanmoise! Plus, I prefer the feeling of being hit without any protection."

"…Did you just say you enjoy being hit?"

"…No."

"Yes, you did."

"Did not." Silence. "So, Aqua, want to try it?" She looked at our Arch-priest, whose face was still hidden in her arms.

"Hey, don't just sit there blubbering—say something! We're talking about your level, here!" I reached out and was about to smack her on the shoulder—

But that's when I noticed…

"*...snooooore...*"

She'd tired herself out from crying and fallen asleep.

Was she a goddess or a toddler?

7

We were on a hill outside town.

It was a communal cemetery for those who died poor or without anyone to bury them. Interment was the custom here—no coffin, just straight in the ground.

Our quest was to deal with the undead monsters that were plaguing the graveyard.

It was almost dusk. We'd pitched camp nearby and were waiting for dark.

"Hey, Kazuma! I had dibs on that meat! We've got some perfectly good grilled vegetables right here—eat some!"

"That cabbage hunt kind of killed my interest in vegetables. I'm always afraid they're going to fly away or jump out of the fire while I'm trying to cook them."

We'd set up a small grill off the cemetery grounds and were making dinner while we waited. It might seem like a lax thing to do when we were ostensibly hunting monsters, but this time our mission was on a low-level creature called a Zombie Maker. They were a kind of evil spirit that controlled zombies. The Zombie Maker commandeered the best corpse and had several undead lieutenants.

We took the quest because we'd heard even novice parties could take on Zombie Makers. Maybe it would be less risky for the unarmored Darkness, as well.

My stomach pleasantly full, I took some powdered coffee and dumped it into a mug. I used a simple magic spell called Create Water to fill it up, then another called Kindle to start a fire to heat it. These were functions of the Basic Magic I'd learned from a Wizard at the cabbage hunt.

Kindle, as the name implied, was used to start fires. You couldn't hurt anyone with it, but it was sure more convenient than a lighter.

Megumin held out her empty mug with a perplexed look.

"Could I have some water, too, please? I am surprised, though, Kazuma. You know even more spells than I do. Most people skip over Basic Magic, but you make it look rather useful."

I chanted Create Water over Megumin's cup.

"I thought that was what Basic Magic was for. Oh yeah. *Create Earth!* What's this one do?" I held out my palm, which was full of fine soil. Basic Magic encompassed spells relating to all four elements, but only the earth spell left me without any idea what to do with it.

"Oh…I have heard it is especially rich soil in which to grow things. That is all."

Aqua piped up at that: "Growing things, huh? How about it, sir Kazuma, planning to switch jobs to a Farmer? You can make your own fields *and* do your own irrigation! Why, you were practically born for it! Pffft hee-hee-hee!"

I pointed my soil-filled right hand at Aqua and made a gesture with my left. "*Wind Breath!*"

"Eeeeyah! G-gaah! My eyeees…"

A gust of wind blew the dirt straight into Aqua's face. The goddess and her sand-filled eyes writhed on the ground.

"Huh, so that's how you use it."

"No, no, it isn't! That is not how you are supposed to use it! How come you are better at beginner magic than an actual Wizard, anyway?"

8

"I feel a chill. Kazuma, didn't the quest say we were looking for a Zombie Maker? I don't think it's that simple… I have a feeling a much worse kind of undead is waiting for us…," Aqua said quaveringly.

The moon had risen; it was late in the night.

"Hey, don't say that. You'll jinx us. We're here to take out one Zombie Maker. Then we rebury the zombies, head back to the stable, and go to sleep. And if anything *weird* happens and things don't go according to plan, we'll skip right to going home. Okay?"

Everyone nodded.

It was almost time. We began to walk toward the graveyard, with me on point, using the Sense Foe skill I'd learned from Chris.

Aqua's words bothered me, but not too much. She was always spouting pointless nonsense, after all.

Well, *almost* always…

…Huh?

"I feel kind of a tingle. Sense Foe is working. There's one, two… three?"

Huh? That was too many.

Granted, we'd heard a Zombie Maker could have two or three zombie underlings. This was within the margin of error.

Just as I was thinking that, a bluish-white light shone in the middle of the cemetery.

…*What was that?*

The light was weirdly, wondrously blue. It seemed oddly far-off, and it looked like a magic circle. And standing next to the circle was a black-robed figure.

"Odd… I do not believe…that is a Zombie Maker," Megumin whispered uncertainly.

Several human forms milled about near the robed person.

"Do we go in? It may not be a Zombie Maker, but anyone in a graveyard at this time of night is an undead for sure. So as long as we've got our Arch-priest with us, we'll be fine."

Darkness was fidgeting, holding her great sword against her chest.

Calm down already, you.

Then Aqua seemed to lose it.

"Ahhhhhh!" she screamed suddenly, and then, before I could figure out what she was thinking, she leaped up and dashed toward the robed figure.

"Wha—? Hey, wait!"

She didn't seem to hear me. Instead, as she neared the mysterious character, she pointed a finger at it accusingly.

"How dare a Lich show her face here so nonchalantly?! You'll pay for this!"

A Lich?

That was a serious undead monster, up on top of the pecking order with vampires and the like. They were known as No-Life Kings: mages who'd mastered the very limits of magic and then abandoned their natural bodies through arcane rituals.

Unlike the average undead, who got that way because of an enduring grudge or powerful attachment to this world, Liches were unhallowed beings who'd deliberately twisted the laws of nature.

Basically, you might expect to see them as a final boss. And here we were looking right at one…

"Eeeek! St-st-stop iiit! Who are you, ma'am?! And why are you trying to break my magic circle?! Stop it! Please stop!"

"Shut your undead mouth! You're up to no good with this circle, I'm sure! Spit it out! Confess!"

Our enemy, the fearsome foe, the final boss, was clinging tearfully to Aqua's legs, trying to keep her from stomping all over the magic circle. The undead that the Lich (?) was controlling did nothing to intervene, just stared blankly at the two of them.

Sooo…what now?

I guess we didn't have a Zombie Maker on our hands, at any rate.

Aqua kept shouting about a Lich, but the supposedly powerful monster looked more like a girl getting bullied by some punk.

"Stop it! Stop, please! This circle helps lost souls find their way to Heaven! Look! You see all those souls ascending from the circle, right?!"

It was true: Bluish-white humanlike figures were appearing from out of nowhere, entering the circle and floating up to the sky in the bluish light.

"You put on a pretty good nice-girl act, Lich! But how about you sit back and let an Arch-priest handle the good-guy stuff?! Why bother with a silly magic ring when I can take care of this whole cemetery at once!"

"Whaaa—? Wait! Stop!" The Lich grew ever more panicked at Aqua's pronouncement. Aqua ignored her. She spread her arms wide and cried:

"*Turn Undead*!"

A white light spread out from Aqua and engulfed the entire graveyard. No sooner had the light touched the Lich's zombies than they vanished. When it reached the human souls who'd gathered in the circle, they, too, disappeared.

And then the light reached the Lich...

"Eeeyaaahh! I-I'm vanishing! Stop! Please stop! I'm going to disappear! I'm not ready to move on yet!"

"Ahhh-ha-ha-ha! Foolish Lich! Defier of the laws of nature! Undead abomination, turning your back on the will of the gods! Soon I'll erase you without a trace!"

"Hey, leave her alone already." I gave Aqua a bop on the back of the head with my sword hilt.

"Huh?! O-owww! What's the big idea?!"

The knock on the head must have broken her concentration, because the white light vanished. Aqua turned on me with her hand to her head and tears in her eyes.

When Darkness and Megumin joined us, I was ignoring Aqua's attempts to strangle me and instead talking to the Lich, who sat shaking on the ground.

"H-hey, are you all right, um...Lich? Can I call you Lich?" I could see that her legs were semitransparent, having started to disappear. They slowly returned to normal, and she unsteadily stood up.

"I-I-I'm all right… Th-that was a close one. Thank you for saving me! Y-you're right—I'm a Lich. My name is Wiz."

As she spoke, she drew back her hood. The moonlight illuminated a face that looked like a normal human's, albeit someone barely twenty years old. Brown hair framed her face. In fact, she was quite lovely.

Somehow, I'd imagined a Lich would look like a skeleton or something.

Wiz's robes were all black, the very picture of an evil mage. Wait—did she still count as an evil mage if she was also a Lich?

"Um, Wiz… What exactly are you doing here? I mean, in a grave-yard in the middle of the night? You said something about sending souls to Heaven? Aqua might have been a little hasty, but I agree that that doesn't sound like something a Lich would do."

"Be careful, Kazuma! If you talk to this rotten apple, you'll become undead, too! Let me cast Turn Undead on her!" Aqua angrily jumped to her feet and made to cast a spell on Wiz.

Wiz ducked behind my back, looking both frightened and dis-mayed, before saying, "Y-yes, I am a Lich, as you can see. A No-Life King. Because I'm a ruler among the undead, I can hear the cries of wandering souls. This is a communal graveyard. Most of the people here were too poor to receive a proper burial. Now they drift among the graves every night, unable to reach Heaven. Since they are under my authority, I come here regularly to help all the little ones who wish to ascend to Heaven."

Gosh, this…this really pulls on my heartstrings.

She was actually a good person. Other than some shopkeepers, maybe the first really decent person I'd met since getting here.

I mean, I guess she wasn't a *person* in the strictest sense.

"That's really admirable, but…isn't that something you should leave for the town's Priests to take care of? Well, Aqua aside."

Wiz glanced uncomfortably at Aqua's frustrated expression before replying—

"Well, you see…the Priests in this town, they…they really care only about money. The poor go forgotten…"

No wonder she looked uncomfortable, with an Arch-priest—Aqua, at that—standing right there.

"Followers of the almighty eris, eh?" I said. "I guess they wouldn't be caught dead holding services in a graveyard for the poor—if you'll excuse the expression."

Everyone looked at Aqua in silence, who awkwardly avoided our collective gaze.

"Well, no changing that, I guess," I went on. "But do you think you could stop summoning all these zombies? We came here thinking we were on the trail of a Zombie Maker, you know."

Wiz seemed uneasy at my words. "Oh…I see… But I don't exactly summon them; when I come here, the spirits who still have bodies simply react to my magical power and come out on their own. If I knew someone was helping the lost souls, though, I wouldn't need to keep coming here…" A long pause. "Oh, isn't there something we can do?"

9

We were on our way home from the cemetery.

"I cannot accept this!" Aqua was still angry.

The sky was already brightening.

"Sorry. She was so sweet. How could you want to destroy her?"

We'd decided to let the Lich go. And we agreed that Aqua, who had plenty of time on her hands anyway, would go to the graveyard every so often to help along its wandering spirits.

Aqua might have been a pretty rotten goddess, but even she seemed to understand that helping lost souls and the undead was her duty.

Even if she complained about not being able to sleep in anymore.

Darkness and Megumin, who'd at first resisted the idea of letting a monster off the hook, relented when they learned that Wiz had never actually attacked anyone.

I looked at the piece of paper Wiz had given me and muttered:

"A Lich just makes her home in this town and nobody minds? Some security."

The piece of paper gave her address. It turned out she was living in Axel, just like we were.

In fact, she was running a little shop that specialized in magic items.

When I said I'd always pictured Liches living in the deepest depths of some dungeon, she replied that dungeons were awfully inconvenient and there was no reason to go out of your way to live in one.

I got what she was saying: Liches were human once, too.

But even though I got it, this place had sure upended most of my assumptions about fantasy worlds. It was nothing like what my games had led me to believe.

"All the same, I am glad things ended peacefully. We may have had Aqua on our side, but we were still facing a Lich. If it had come to a fight, Kazuma and I would have surely died," Megumin said casually. I almost choked.

"Erk! Are Liches really that dangerous? Just how close a call was this?"

"'Close' does not begin to describe it. Liches have extremely high Magic Defense, and only enchanted weapons can harm them. They can inflict a variety of status conditions merely by touching you, or they can absorb your HP and MP. Truly, they are legendary foes. Indeed, what I find perplexing is that Aqua's Turn Undead spell worked on her at all."

Good point. Liches were at the top of the undead heap, after all.

I was happy to take her business card because she said she would teach me some Lich abilities, but…when I went to see her, I figured I'd be sure to bring Aqua with me.

"Kazuma, gimme that business card. I'm gonna get to her house before she does and place a holy barrier around it. That'll show her!"

"L-lay off it, would you…?"

On second thought, maybe I'd leave her at home.

Darkness interrupted my thoughts with a question: "Where does this leave our Zombie Maker quest?"

With a sigh, all of us said at once: "Oh."

Quest failed.

Chapter 3

May the Self-Proclaimed Goddess Have Her First Pressing at This Lake!

1

"Hey, didja hear? They say one of the Demon King's generals moved into that castle on the hill outside town!"

I was in a corner of the Guild tavern. All afternoon I'd been drinking and shooting the breeze with the guy sitting next to me.

Well, *drinking*, yes—but not alcohol. My beverage of choice was Neroid Fizzizz as I chatted with the guy.

What's Neroid, you ask? And Fizzizz, for that matter?

It was a favorite here among those who didn't drink much, so out of curiosity I'd decided to give it a try.

But…

If someone were to ask me if it was any good, I'd have to answer:
Um…I don't know.

But at least I'd figured out what Fizzizz was. The sensation of drinking it was very *fizzizz*.

It wasn't carbonation. I had no idea what *fizzizz* actually meant, but it was definitely the right word.

I drank the last of my Neroid and set it on the table…

"One of the Demon King's generals? That sounds like a pain, but it doesn't have anything to do with us."

"Damn straight." He chuckled at my disinterested, unconcerned response.

There was a surprisingly large number of people just hanging around the Adventurers Guild chatting, and you could hear a lot of interesting things: A dangerous monster had been found in such-and-such place, so you'd better avoid doing quests there for a while. That monster hates the smell of citrus, so if you rub some citrus juice on yourself, it won't attack you. That kind of thing.

Actually, since I'd gotten to this world, I'd had my hands full just trying to make a living. This was the first time I'd done any intelligence gathering like this. In a video game, getting information was one of the most important ways to learn about new story beats. Being part of conversations in the tavern like this made me feel like a real adventurer, and it was terrific.

The man across from me said, "Well anyway, you'd better stay away from the old castle to the north. I dunno what the Demon King's general wants out here. This ain't the Capital or anything. Seein' as he's a general, you suppose he's an ogre or a vampire? Or maybe an arch-demon or a dragon? Whatever. I'm sure he'd wipe out any of our parties in a second. Just steer clear of that castle—for your own sake."

I thanked the man and stood, then turned toward where my own party was sitting, but...

"What? Why are you all looking at me like that?"

Aqua, Darkness, and Megumin were gnawing on vegetable sticks resting in a glass on the middle of the table and watching me.

"No reason," Aqua said with an uneasy shift of her eyes. "I mean, obviously we're not worried that you might join another party or anything."

"Huh...? Look, getting information is Adventuring 101." I sat down at the table with them and reached for a vegetable stick.

The stick dodged out of my reach.

...Sheesh.

"What are you doing, Kazuma?" Aqua gave the table a good smack, causing the vegetable stick to jump in surprise. She grabbed the temporarily immobilized snack and popped it in her mouth.

"Hmm. You seemed to be enjoying yourself. Were you enjoying yourself, Kazuma? You sure looked like you were having a good time, talking to that guy from that other party…"

Megumin slammed her balled-up fist on the table, snatched one of the startled vegetables, and ate it.

"What is this strange new feeling…? Seeing Kazuma so friendly with another party…it gives me a little flutter. A sensation I don't understand. Is it the feeling of being cuckolded…?"

Our resident perv kept up this weird chatter as she flicked the rim of the glass and grabbed one of the sticks.

"What's with you guys? I thought every adventurer tried to catch the latest gossip." As I spoke, I struck the table, then reached out for…

Sproing!

"…Gaaaaaaahhhhhhh!"

"Stop! Stop it! What are you doing to my vegetable sticks? Don't waste food like that!"

Having failed to catch the vegetable stick, I'd instead grabbed the whole glass and was about to fling it against the wall, but a panicked Aqua grabbed my hand.

"You think I'm gonna let a vegetable stick beat me?! And why do the vegetables always run away, huh? Can't they bring us something that's already dead?"

"What are you talking about? Vegetables are just like fish—the fresher, the better. You know how in Japan they sometimes serve fish still alive? It's the same thing."

No, it's not. These are *vegetables*.

I gave up the idea of eating these.

"Huh… Fine. Forget vegetables for now. There's something I want to ask you guys. I've been thinking about what skill to learn when my level goes up next time. Frankly, this party is totally unbalanced, and since I can learn anything, I'd like to try to fill some of the holes in our makeup." I paused. "So, what kinds of skills do you guys have?"

If you wanted to complete quests efficiently, it was important to make sure your party members' abilities complemented one another. That was why I'd brought this up.

"I have Physical Resistance and Magic Resistance, as well as Resistance skills for every status condition. Oh, and Decoy, too."

"...You don't want to take something like Two-Handed Sword and up your Accuracy a bit?"

"Nope. Not to brag, but I have high HP and Strength. If I were able to actually hit monsters most of the time, I might defeat them before they ever got a chance to hit me in return. I could hold back and let them attack me on purpose, but...it's not the same. It's like...to go in there swinging my sword as hard as I can, but it's just not enough, and they overpower me...that feels so *good*, you know?"

"No, I don't. That's enough out of you."

"Mm...! *He* asks me for my opinion, and then *he* shoots me down...!" Darkness was blushing, and she'd started to breathe heavily. I ignored her.

When I turned to Megumin, she cocked her head quizzically.

"I have explosion-related skills, obviously. The spell Explosion, plus skills that boost the power of explosive magics, along with high-speed incantation and so forth. Everything I need to release the most powerful magical blasts. That is all that has ever guided my choice of skills, and all that ever will."

"And I don't suppose you have any intention of learning Intermediate Magic."

"No."

So she wasn't going to be any help, either.

"Let's see, I have..."

"Don't care."

"Whaaat?!"

I shut down Aqua before she could begin listing her skills. I was sure it was just party trick, party trick, party trick.

Sheesh...

"This party is completely uncoordinated. Maybe I really should look for a new group..."

All three of them recoiled at my muttered suggestion.

2

It had been several days since the urgent cabbage-harvesting quest. We'd recently sold all the cabbages we'd collected, and the adventurers had finally gotten their payment for the harvest...

"Have a look, Kazuma! I got enough of a reward from the cabbage hunt to have them improve my armor a bit while it was in the shop. What do you think?"

Amid the commotion of every adventurer in the Guild Hall trying to claim their cabbage payout, Darkness nearly glowed as she showed off her armor. All I could say was...

"That thing looks like it was tricked out for some rich kid who wouldn't know armor from a hole in the ground."

"...You never say anything nicely, do you, Kazuma? You know, even I just want to hear a kind word every once in a while." She looked uncharacteristically unhappy.

Well, how was I supposed to know?

More important...

"I don't have time to coddle you right now. There's a bigger problem on our hands. You need to do something about that freak over there. She's turning out to be worse than you."

"Ohhh... Ohhhh! I can't *staaaand* it! This manatite staff is just *throbbing* with magical power... Ohhh! Ohhh!" Megumin was rubbing her cheek up and down the new staff she'd had made. Apparently, if you constructed it with a rare metal called manatite, it boosted the staff's attack power. Megumin had used the generous cabbage reward to get such a manatite staff, and she'd been acting this way all day. She was convinced her explosions would be that much more powerful now.

Her Explosion spell was overkill as it was. What could she possibly do with *more* power? Wasn't there some more helpful magic she could learn? I knew better than to ask her that, though. In her present state, I really just wanted to stay away from her.

I'd gotten my reward, too, and I was riding high.

We had Darkness, who'd taken on the monsters that had come after the cabbage.

Megumin, who'd blown them all up.

And Aqua, who'd gone off after whatever vegetables she could find and paid no attention to what the rest of us were doing.

We'd decided to split the reward not evenly but proportionally, based on how many cabbages each of us had caught. It was Aqua's idea—since she'd gotten the most after me.

And now she was waiting to reap the rewards of her brilliant idea…

"Whaaaaat?! Hold on—what is going on here?!"

Her shout echoed throughout the Guild Hall.

Uh-oh…

Sure enough, Aqua was at the clerk's counter, fuming. She had the clerk by the collar and was giving her a tongue-lashing.

"Fifty thousand measly eris? Do you know how many cabbages I caught?! I can tell you it was more than that!"

"I-I-I'm very sorry to tell you this, but…"

"What?!"

"…Miss Aqua, most of what you brought back was lettuce…"

"Why was there lettuce flying around, too?!"

"I-I'm sure I don't know, ma'am…"

It sounded like Aqua had gotten considerably less money than she'd expected. Perhaps she figured it would be futile to abuse the staff any further: She came over to me with her hands behind her back and an ingratiating smile on her face.

"Oh, Kazuma, my *friend*... How much did you make on this quest?"

"A million even."

All three of my companions' jaws dropped.

It was true: That quest had come out of thin air and made me a minor *nouveau riche*.

I'd managed to collect a number of especially high-quality cabbages packed with XP. Just another benefit of good Luck, I guess.

"You know, oh great Kazuma, I've always thought you were one of the...uh...well, the *nicest* people I've ever met..."

"If you can't think of anything nice to say, don't force yourself. Anyway, I've already decided how I'm gonna spend this money, so I'm not sharing."

Aqua's smile froze as I pulled the rug out from under her.

"But Kazumaaaaaa! I was so sure this quest was gonna pay out, I spent all my money! I ran up a hundred-thousand-eris tab at the bar here! My reward isn't nearly enough to cover that!"

I peeled the beseeching Aqua off me. Why did she never think ahead? I rubbed my aching temples.

"Not my problem. You're the one who said everyone should get 'just what they earned and no more.' Anyway, I want to find an actual place to live. How can we be serious adventurers if we spend our entire careers renting a stable?"

Most adventurers didn't own houses. They traveled around too much for that. Then again, with the exception of a handful of successful questers, most lived a hand-to-mouth existence and couldn't support a residence.

Frankly, in light of the human resources I had available, I'd given up on ever defeating the Demon King. Let the other guys who'd been sent here before me deal with him—the ones who'd picked incredible special abilities or awesome equipment or whatever.

I was sitting here as an Adventurer, the lowest job class, something any loser could do. My stats weren't even that good. Certainly nothing like people who'd been training their whole lives for this work. I was barely better than average.

I would be happy to adventure just enough to satisfy my curiosity, in relative safety, and then retire to a nice, comfortable existence. So I'd planned to use my reward to lease a place or maybe even buy a little cabin if the price was right.

Aqua had attached herself to me, looking ready to burst into tears.

"Nooooo! Kazuma, pleeeease! Lend me some money! Just enough to pay my tab! Look, Kazuma, I know you're a boy, and I can hear the rustling from your side of the stable in the middle of the night sometimes, so I know why you want to hurry up and get a place where you can have some privacy! But pleeeease! Just fifty thousand! Fifty thousand is plenty! I'm begging youuu!"

"Geez! All right! Fifty thousand, a hundred thousand—I don't care! Just shut up already!"

3

"Kazuma, hurry, we must find some monsters! Ideally, a great many weaklings! I want to try my new staff!"

Such was the request Megumin suddenly brought me.

Hmm.

"Sure. I haven't had time to try out the skills I learned since we went on that Zombie Maker quest. How about we find something nice and easy to do?"

"No, let's do something profitable! I used every eris I had to pay my tab, so I can't afford lunch today!"

"I say we should find a powerful opponent! Something of immense strength, whose every crushing blow will feel sooo good…!"

Sheesh. I knew everyone wanted to do their own thing sometimes, but this was ridiculous.

"Well, let's see what's on the board first and go from there." At my suggestion, we all crowded around to see the quests. Where…

"What's going on? There's almost no posts here." Usually there was hardly space on the board, but today only a few pieces of paper hung there.

And what was there was…

"Kazuma! I've found our quest! A giant bear called Blackfang has been spotted in the mountains…"

"No way! What's going on here? All these quests are, like, impossible!" Everything on the board was wildly out of our league.

A Guild employee approached us.

"Ahem… I'm very sorry about that. A person appearing to be one of the Demon King's generals recently took up residence in a nearby castle, and, well…all the weaker monsters are keeping out of sight, meaning much less work for adventurers. A division of Knights will be sent from the Capital next month to deal with the emergency, but until then, we expect mostly high-level quests…"

The penniless Aqua gave a cry of despair at the employee's apologetic words. "Wh-whyyyyy?!"

For once, I had to agree with her.

"Arrrgh… Why'd that stupid general have to move in now? I don't care what rank he is, if he's undead, then just leave him to me!" Aqua grumbled with brimming eyes as she flipped through the classifieds.

Everyone else seemed to be feeling the same way. I'd never seen so many adventurers drinking in the middle of the day. The mood was despondent.

What did a general of the Demon King want out here, anyway? Most of the adventurers in Axel weren't that much stronger than we were. Of course there were some more powerful parties—but even they weren't all that impressive.

Axel was a starter town, a place people came to begin their careers. A general of the Demon King was the sort of enemy you'd expect to encounter at the end of a game, not the beginning. We could barely handle some overgrown frogs. The entire town together probably wasn't a match for whoever was in that castle.

4

"Until the Knights and do-gooders from the Capital arrive next month, we're not going to get any real work done…"

"So it appears. And since you have no quests to occupy your time, why not accompany me?"

Megumin and I were just outside town.

There were no dangerous enemies around at the moment. All the little monsters were off cowering in fear at the presence of the Demon King's general.

Megumin and I had gone out for a walk. I couldn't take on any quests, and she had nothing to blow up with her explosions, so we were both feeling pretty down. Megumin made it a daily ritual to fire off one magical explosion. I hoped I wasn't stuck babysitting her every single day for the next month. I had told her to go by herself, but she'd replied that there'd be no one to carry her home.

In a spot nearby, I suggested Megumin perform her magic. "How about over there? Just let one off, and we can get out of here."

She shook her head.

"This won't do. If I'm not far enough from town, the guards will yell at me again."

"'Again'? What, did people complain about the noise or something?"

She gave a short nod.

No choice, then. I wasn't thrilled to be leaving the area without a weapon, but there weren't supposed to be any monsters around, anyway.

It wouldn't hurt to see the wider world just a bit.

Come to think of it, I'd hardly done any touring since getting to this world. When I left town, it was always to hunt monsters for a quest. Just calmly wandering around like this was…

"…? Hey, what's that? An abandoned castle?"

It stood on a far-off hill: an old redoubt slowly crumbling away.

It looked like it was probably haunted…

"I don't like the feel of that place," I muttered. "I bet there's ghosts in there or something…"

"It is perfect!" Megumin exclaimed. "I can blow it up as thoroughly as I wish, and no one will be bothered!" And she happily began preparing her spell.

A pleasant breeze blew across the hill.

It was quiet. It was calm. And then I heard Megumin's chanting on the wind…

That was how Megumin and I passed the time each day.

Aqua, without an eris to her name, had taken on a part-time job, and Darkness had gone back to her hometown to train. Megumin had nothing better to do, so every day we would go to that abandoned castle and set off a magical explosion.

It might be in the evening, with a cold rain falling.

Or in the afternoon, after a quiet meal.

Even during a lovely early-morning walk.

At some point each day, Megumin would unleash her magic on that castle…

I went with her each time and had even gotten to the point where I could tell how good the day's explosion had been.

"*Explosion*!!"

"Ooh, that was a good one! You could feel the vibrations in your bones, but then the way the shock wave came a moment later and kind of brushed your skin… I'm always curious why that castle never seems the worse for wear after you blow it up. But, oh well. Nice one!"

"'Nice one!' Heh-heh. Kazuma, you have gained no small appreciation for the explosive path. Your appraisal of today's blast was nothing short of poetic. How about it, Kazuma? Might you seriously consider learning explosive magic?"

"Hmm… I admit it's tempting, but with our party's current makeup, I don't think a second Wizard would be a good idea. Maybe I can look forward to learning Explosion when I've finally retired from adventuring."

We laughed together as we chatted. How many points would we give today's explosion? Well, the volume was a little low, but the quality of the sound was so good—we went over it piece by piece, chatting away.

5

Thus we spent a week in pleasant explosions. Then, one morning…

"*Urgent! Urgent!* All adventurers, please equip your weapons and items and prepare for battle at the town gate!" The familiar sound of an emergency announcement echoed through the streets. We dutifully grabbed our gear and headed for the town square.

When we arrived in the press of adventurers gathered in front of the main gate, we saw a monster standing there casually, oozing terror.

A Dullahan.

Dullahans are headless riders, harbingers of death; they inspire only despair. They're a form of undead whose physical strength and special abilities surpass anything they possessed while alive.

The creature that stood at the town gate looked like a Knight in pitch-black armor. His own head rested under his left arm, and before an entire town's worth of adventurers, he held out the helmeted visage. A muffled voice issued from it:

"I am the general of the Demon King, who lately took up residence in a castle near this town…"

The head gradually began to shudder.

"A-a-and *every single day*—!! Every *damn* day, one of you recalcitrant idiots comes and sets off a magical explosion in my castle! Who is it?! Tell meeee!"

I guess he was angry.

The Dullahan's exasperated yell set the adventurers around me murmuring. No one there had the slightest idea what was going on.

If nothing else, it was clear the Dullahan was the reason we'd all been called out in such a hurry.

"A magical explosion…?"

"Do we know anyone who can use Explosion?"

"Explosion, huh…?"

One by one, the faces in the crowd turned to Megumin, next to me.

Megumin promptly turned to a young Wizard girl standing beside her.

I followed her lead, and soon everyone was looking at the girl instead.

"Wh-what's going on? Why's everyone staring at me? I—I can't use Explosion!" the object of our suspicion said with a touch of panic.

…Wait a second. *We've* been setting off an explosion at an old castle every day…

Could it possibly be…?

I cast a sidelong glance at Megumin. She'd broken out in a cold sweat.

Apparently she'd had the same thought I had.

Finally Megumin sighed, made a face, and stepped out from the crowd. As she did so, the collected adventurers moved aside for her.

The Dullahan stood in front of the town gate. Megumin stopped about ten meters away from him. First I, then Darkness and Aqua, stepped up behind her. At the sight of the undead creature, Aqua had gotten a look much like a parent upset with a misbehaving child. She'd been avidly watching the whole scene—perhaps an enraged Dullahan was just that rare a sight.

"*You!*" he said. "Are you the fool who keeps setting off those blasted explosions?! If you're looking for a fight with one of the Demon King's generals, then at least have the guts to storm my castle yourself! And if that *isn't* what you want, stay in your little town and cower! Why resort to petty harassment? I knew this was a town full of fledglings, so I left you in peace—but I see this only invited your arrogance! *Boom, boom, boom, boom, boom*, every day! Are you insane?!"

The Dullahan's helmet vibrated with the anger he'd stored up over a week of explosions.

Megumin shivered a little, obviously intimidated—but then she threw back her mantle and declared:

"I am Megumin! Arch-wizard and master of Explosion!"

"Megumin? What kind of a name is that? Are you making fun of me?"

"I am not!"

She apparently hadn't been expecting the Dullahan to shoot her down. But she quickly collected herself.

"I am of the Crimson Magic Clan and the greatest magic-user in Axel Town! Those explosions were a stratagem to draw you out, O general of the Demon King! Your luck ran out the moment you came to this town alone!" She waved her staff at him menacingly.

Behind her, I whispered to Darkness and Aqua. "Can somebody tell me what she's talking about? She swore she had to let off an explosion every day or she'd die, so I took her to that stupid castle. When did it become a 'stratagem'?"

"Good question. And when did she become this town's greatest magic-user?"

"Shush back there! I have not set off an explosion yet today, and an entire crowd of adventurers backs me up. I am in a position of strength here—and I will see to this town's safety!"

I guess Megumin could hear us whispering, because she blushed a little even as she stood posted with her staff thrust forward.

The Dullahan, for some reason, actually seemed to be taking her at face value.

"Oh-ho, a member of the Crimson Magic Clan? I see, I see. So that ridiculous name you gave wasn't just to mock me."

"Hey! If you have something to say about the name my parents gave me, then let's hear it!" Megumin said hotly, but her foe hardly paid her any mind. In fact, he seemed to find the entire crowd barely worth his notice. The general of the Demon King was no more interested in us than a hawk in a gaggle of chicks.

"Hmph, never mind. I did not come to this town to trade barbs with children. I am in this area for research purposes, and I will be living in that castle for the foreseeable future. So desist your magical explosions, you understand?"

"You, sir, might as well order me to die. For we of the Crimson Magic Clan perish if we do not let off an explosion every day!"

"Wh-what? I've never heard such nonsense! If you're going to lie, at least make up something plausible!"

I didn't know what to do. Honestly, I was kind of enjoying watching the two of them go at it. I could see Aqua, too, looking eagerly at Megumin as she nearly frothed at the monster's insults.

The Dullahan placed his head on his right palm, and then—rather nimbly—gave an annoyed shrug.

"So you have no intention of giving up your magic, do you? Though I have relinquished my body to a demon, I was once a Knight. Slaughtering the weak holds no interest for me. But if you insist on bothering me in my home every day—well, I have an idea of how to deal with you…"

Megumin began to back away from the Dullahan, who seemed more and more dangerous.

But to my surprise, she was smiling.

"You, sir, are the one bothering us! Ever since you arrived, we have been unable to work!" She smirked. "Heh. I think you had best escape while you can. For we have an undead specialist among us! Milady, if you please!"

All that grand posturing—and now Megumin had neatly handed off the whole thing to Aqua.

…Sheesh.

Aqua, clearly pleased to be called "milady," stepped up to face the Dullahan. "Looks like it's up to me, then! I don't care if you're the Demon King's general or whatever, it's your bad luck you showed up while I was here! An undead who comes in the middle of the day—you're practically begging me to send you to the netherworld. It's your fault we can't get any decent quests around here! Now—prepare yourself!" She thrust one hand out toward the Dullahan. The adventurers gathered behind us gave a collective gulp.

The Dullahan looked intrigued. He turned his head to face Aqua and held it out toward her. It seemed to be his way of showing he was getting serious.

"Oh-ho, what have we here? No mere Priest, but an Arch-priest? I am a general of the Demon King. Shall a low-level Arch-priest in a starter town banish me from this realm? Do you think I have not prepared countermeasures for Priests far more powerful than you? Ah, but perhaps this will be a good opportunity to torment my little Crimson friend…"

Quicker than Aqua could chant her spell, he pointed with his left hand at Megumin. Then he bellowed:

"I pronounce death upon you! In one week's time, you shall die!"

In the same instant as the Dullahan intoned his curse, Darkness grabbed Megumin by the collar and threw the Wizard behind her.

"Wha—?!" Megumin cried. "D-Darkness!" For an instant, Darkness's body shone with a black light.

A death curse! Damn!

"Darkness!" I said. "Are you all right?! Are you hurt?!" She was opening and closing her hand as if to make sure it still worked.

"Hmm… It looks like I'm…fine," she said calmly.

But I'd heard the Dullahan: *In one week's time, you shall die.*

Aqua was busily looking Darkness over when the Dullahan

exclaimed triumphantly, "The curse appears as nothing now! This is not quite what I planned, but with the bonds of fellowship you adventurers share, it may be even better! Listen, you Crimson whelp. Your Crusader will die a week from this day. Heh-heh! You can watch her stew in the terror of her impending demise—and know that it is your fault! Watch her suffer for seven days, and rue what you have done! Bwa-ha-haa! If you had only listened to me…!"

At his words, Megumin paled, and Darkness moaned with excitement.

"H-how devious! You have placed this curse of death upon me—and in order to break it, we must do *whatever* you want! Isn't that right?!"

"Huh?"

The Dullahan seemed completely flummoxed by Darkness's reaction. I had no idea what she was talking about, either.

…All right, I didn't *want* to have any idea.

"Hrgh… I am daunted by no curse…a-and yet… Kazuma! What shall we do?! Look at the terrible eyes burning within that Dullahan's helm! Those are the eyes of one who would take me to his castle as his sex prisoner and force me to do all kinds of freaky hard-core porno stuff if I want to break this curse!"

"…*Huh?*" said the Dullahan, having clearly not expected to be called out as a pervert in front of the whole town. I felt a little bad for him.

"Well, you may be the master of my body, but you will never be the master of my heart! A female Knight—prisoner in a castle, slave to the vile demands of the Demon King's minion! What should I *do*, Kazuma?! Who could have foreseen things would turn so hot! I don't want to go—I cannot bear it!—and yet, I have no choice! I'll resist him for as long as I can… Don't try to stop me! Farewell now, my friends!"

"Whaaat?!"

"Stoppit already! That's obviously not what he has in mind!"

I grabbed Darkness's arm and held her back from her headlong dash toward our enemy. The Dullahan was palpably relieved.

"A-anyway. I hope you've learned your lesson and won't blow up my home anymore! And you, Magic child—if you want to break that Crusader's curse, come to my castle! If you survive to reach my chamber on the top floor, I shall lift the curse. But know this: A legion of Undead Knights guards my castle! I will be most curious to see if you and your fledgling friends ever reach me! Bwa-ha-ha-ha…ha-ha-ha-ha-haaaa!"

Still cackling, the Dullahan walked out the gate, mounted his headless horse, and rode off to his castle.

6

The crowd of adventurers stood silently, seemingly overwhelmed by the turn of events.

I felt the same way.

Next to me, Megumin clutched her staff, pale and trembling.

Alone, she made to walk through the town gate.

"Hey, where do you think you're going? What have you got in mind?" I grabbed her mantle. Megumin just pulled harder as she tried to walk away. She didn't look back as she answered:

"This is my fault. I am simply going to go to that castle, let off one good explosion right in that Dullahan's face, and break Darkness's curse."

Like she was going to manage anything by herself.

Actually, come to think of it…

"I'm going with you, obviously. By yourself, you'd probably use up your explosion on some piddling guard, and then what? You were too dim to even notice we were blowing up the castle of the Demon King's general."

Megumin stared at me for a moment, then her shoulders relaxed as if resigned.

"Fine, come with me, then. But that monster mentioned a legion of Undead Knights. Your sword is not going to be very effective against such enemies. Today, you must rely on my magic." A slight smile flitted across her face.

Undead Knights presumably wore armor, like their living counterparts. My cheap sword wasn't going to scratch them. But I had an idea.

"I can use my Sense Foe skill to tell where the enemies are. As we go through the castle, I'll track them, and then we can jump them with my Ambush skill. Or maybe we could go there once a day and take out all the enemies on one floor of the castle with Explosion. Then we go home and come back the next day. We could probably clear the whole place in a week, right?"

Megumin brightened a bit, perhaps seeing a glimmer of hope in my strategy. The two of us turned to Darkness.

"Hey, Darkness! We're gonna lift that curse, I guarantee it! So you just—"

"*Sacred Dispel!*"

Aqua's incantation interrupted my attempt to encourage Darkness. Darkness's body shone with a faint light.

Aqua's cheerful face was a stark contrast to the despondent-looking Crusader.

"Some Dullahan's little curses don't stand a chance against me! How about that, huh? I can totally act like a real Priest sometimes!"

Megumin and I looked at her.

"Huh…?" we said.

And here Megumin and I had been just starting to get excited. Way to take the wind out of our sails, Aqua.

7

We passed an uneventful week after our brush with the Demon King's general.

*   *   *

"I need a quest! Even a hard one! Let's go on a quest!"

"Huh?" Megumin and I were startled by Aqua's sudden outburst, and less than pleased.

Except Aqua, our party's purses were overflowing. We certainly didn't want to go out and work now, with only high-level quests available.

"I don't mind," Darkness said. "But Aqua, you and I alone rather... lack firepower." She glanced significantly at Megumin and me. Well, she could give us all the significant glances she wanted. There was no need for the two of us to go on any dangerous quests.

Aqua could see we weren't biting, and she began to plead.

"Pleeease! I'm sooo sick of doing part-time work every single day! The store owner gets mad at me if there's even one croquette still left at the end of the day! I promise I'll be helpful this time! I prooomise!"

Megumin and I looked at each other.

"Geez, all right already. Fine, go have a look at the board and see if there's anything worthwhile. If you can find something decent, we'll go with you."

Aqua dashed off happily to the quest board.

"Kazuma, could you perhaps take a look at the board, too? I have a bad feeling about leaving Aqua to pick something by herself..."

"She's right. Though I personally wouldn't mind a quest that got us beat up a little..."

The girls were right, and I knew it. I went over to the quest board with mounting dread. I stood behind Aqua as she diligently scrutinized the quests. She didn't notice me, only continued to study the pieces of paper tacked to the board. Finally she picked one and pulled it off.

"Okay!"

"What's okay?! Do you even know what you're getting us into?!"

I grabbed the paper from her.

*   *   *

MANTICORE/GRIFFIN HUNT — A MANTICORE AND A GRIFFIN ARE FIGHTING OVER TERRITORY HERE, MAKING THE AREA VERY DANGEROUS. SEEKING ADVENTURER(S) TO HUNT BOTH MONSTERS AND END THE FEUD. REWARD: 500,000 ERIS.

"Are you insane?!" I shouted, and put the paper back where she'd found it.

Good thing I'd come to check on her. She'd almost gotten us into a lot of trouble.

"Why are you so upset? There're only two of them! We get them in one place and let Megumin do her thing! Boom! We go home. Sheesh! Forget it."

Yeah, great plan. And I supposed it was up to me to figure out how to lure two magical, feuding monsters to the same spot.

Just as I was considering taking the quest and sending Aqua off to handle it alone, she came up and started pulling excitedly on my sleeve.

"Hey, look! Check this one out!" I looked at the quest she was pointing to.

LAKE CLEANSING — THE NEARBY LAKE, WHICH PROVIDES MUCH OF THE TOWN'S WATER, HAS BECOME IMPURE, AND BRUTAL ALLIGATORS HAVE TAKEN UP RESIDENCE THERE. SEEKING PURIFICATION OF THE LAKE. THE MONSTERS WILL LEAVE IF THE WATER IS CLEANSED, SO HUNTING THEM IS NOT NECESSARY. NOTE: PARTY MUST INCLUDE A PRIEST WHO HAS MASTERED PURIFICATION MAGIC. REWARD: 300,000 ERIS.

"…Do you know how to purify water?"

Aqua snorted. "Now who's being dumb? Just who do you think I am? Think about my name, look at my outfit, and tell me—what do you *think* I rule over?"

"Party tricks?"

"Wrong, you hikiNEET! Water! The pale blue eyes? The hair? Do these things mean nothing to you?"

I guess I can see the connection.

Three hundred thousand eris just to clean up a little water—it was definitely tempting. Especially the fact that we didn't have to fight anything.

"Fine, let's take it. Heck, if it's just water purification, you can handle it on your own, can't you? Then you could keep the reward all to yourself."

But Aqua hesitated.

"Y-yeah…I guess I could… But those monsters probably won't just sit by and watch me purify their lake. I need someone to protect me from them until I'm done."

Aha…

But "Brutal Alligators"—presumably they were some kind of alligator, right? That sounded bad.

"How long does it take you to purify water, anyway? Five minutes?"

If it was quick enough, we might be able to make do with one good explosion from Megumin.

Aqua shook her head. "Maybe half a day?"

"It might as well take forever!"

So we were supposed to guard her for upward of twelve hours against monsters whose name alone sounded like trouble. I made to put the paper back…

"Aww, nooo! Please! There aren't any other good quests! Oh pleeease help me with this, Kazumaaa!"

I looked at Aqua, clinging to my arm to keep me from returning the quest, and suddenly thought to ask:

"How do you do the whole cleansing thing, anyway?"

"Huh? I just touch the water and keep using Purification magic… Why?"

I see. She had to physically touch the water. For a second I'd thought…

Well, wait.

"All right, Aqua. I think I know how you can do your ritual—no risk, no problem. Wanna give it a try?"

8

The lake in question was a large body of water not far from town.

This was one of the town's major water sources; a small river flowed from this lake all the way to Axel. The snowmelt from mountains immediately bordering the lake was what kept it full.

I could see it: The water was somehow cloudy and stagnant, just as the request had said.

I'd thought maybe monsters liked clean water, just like humans, but I guess not.

As I gazed out at the lake, Aqua's trembling voice came from behind me—

"Are… Are we really gonna go through with this?" She seemed extremely ill at ease.

But my plan was airtight. What could she possibly object to?

"I feel like some rare monster you're going to sell to the Guild…or the circus," Aqua said. She was sitting cross-legged in a steel cage—not unlike the kind you might use to hold a rare monster.

I was going to take the cage, with Aqua inside, and dump it into the lake.

At first I'd thought she could just sit safely in the cage at the lakeside and do her magic, but when I found out she had to touch the water for the magic to work, I revised my plan.

Being the goddess of water, Aqua could, she said, be submerged all day without even getting tense, let alone drowning. And—again, so she said—even if she wasn't actively using the Purification magic, the water would gradually be cleansed just by her presence in it.

I guess she's just that holy. She is a goddess, after all, even if you'd never guess it.

We'd borrowed the cage from the Guild; they had it on hand for quests that required prey be captured rather than killed.

The cage didn't need to go all the way to the bottom of the lake—useless cargo and all. It just needed to sit deep enough for Aqua to touch the water. Since the cage was big enough to carry a monster, Aqua could just stay in the middle of it, out of range of any attacks.

The Guild employee said the monsters would leave the area when the water was purified, but just in case they wouldn't leave Aqua alone, we'd attached some sturdy chains.

A steel cage isn't light, so in town we'd borrowed a horse to drag it out here. In an emergency, we could have the horse pull it back by the chains.

We shoved the cage past the lake's edge, the water rising until it reached Aqua's legs and bottom.

The rest of us just needed to wait nearby.

Aqua hugged her knees and muttered dejectedly:

"I feel like a tea bag you've left to steep…"

9

Purification plan in motion, we'd set Aqua in the water at the edge of the lake. Two hours passed, but there was no sign of any monsters.

Megumin, Darkness, and I watched and waited in a spot about twenty meters from Aqua.

Aqua sat in the partially flooded cage. I called out to her:

"Hey, Aqua! How's the cleanup going? Not getting cold in that lake water? If you need to go to the bathroom or anything, just tell me! I'll let you out of there!"

She shouted back:

"It's going fine! And I don't need the toilet! Arch-priests don't go to the bathroom!"

Whatever. She sounded like a washed-up idol.

I'd thought sitting there in the water for hours might be a problem, but apparently not.

"It looks like she is doing all right. Incidentally, the people of the Crimson Magic Clan do not use the bathroom, either," Megumin said. As if I'd asked her.

She and Aqua both had bottomless stomachs. I wondered where it all went.

"I'm a Crusader, and we…we…hrr…"

"Don't get into a not-pissing contest with those two, Darkness. One of these days we're gonna get a quest that takes more than a few hours. Then we'll see who does and doesn't go to the bathroom."

"P-please stop it! Crimson Magic Clan members really do not use the toilet. But I will apologize, so please stop… Strange, though, that there seems to be no sign of the Brutal Alligators. Well, we can only hope they leave us alone," Megumin said. A line like that was an invitation to raise an event flag if I ever heard one.

No sooner had she spoken than ripples appeared in the water.

It wasn't any bigger than a normal Earth alligator—but it sure *seemed* different. It was a monster, no doubt.

"K-Kazuma! Something's coming! A wh-whole bunch of somethings!"

Apparently the alligators here traveled in packs.

—Four hours into the purification process—

At first, Aqua had simply sat in the water, relying on her divine powers to purify it, but now she was desperately chanting spells, too.

"*Purification! Purification! Purification!!*"

The crowd of alligators surrounded Aqua's cage and began gnawing on it.

"*Purification*! *Purification*! Y-you know, my cage is c-creaking! I-it's squeaking! Do somethiiiing!"

But there wasn't much we *could* do. With Aqua right in the midst of the monsters, Megumin's Explosion wasn't a sound plan.

"Aqua! If you're ready to throw in the towel, just say the word! I'll have the horse pull the chains and we'll get you out of there!"

I'd been shouting similar advice for some time, but Aqua had thus far refused to give up on her quest.

"N-no way! We'll have wasted all this time, *and* we won't get any reward! *Purification*! *Purification*! E-eeeek! Did you hear that crack?! That is definitely not a sound you want to hear from the bars protecting you!"

The swarm of alligators mobbing Aqua's cage didn't so much as look at us.

Darkness took in the scene and sighed.

"I kind of wish I was in that cage…"

"…Don't get any ideas."

—Seven hours into the purification process—

The battered cage sat glumly in the lake. It was covered in alligator bite marks.

The alligators themselves had turned tail and headed for the mountains. Maybe because we'd finished purifying the lake.

I couldn't hear Aqua chanting her spells anymore.

Actually, it had been almost an hour since I'd last heard her voice rising from within the crowd of monsters.

"Hey, Aqua, you all right? Looks like all the alligators swam off somewhere."

The rest of us approached, trying to get a look at Aqua.

"…*Hic*…*sniff*… Waaah…!"

If she was going to sit there hugging her knees and crying, she should've just dropped the quest.

On the other hand…I guess, for once, I could understand the reaction.

"Hey. If you're done purifying the place, let's go home. I talked to Darkness and Megumin, and we all agreed we don't need a reward for this one. You can keep the three hundred grand all to yourself."

Aqua didn't look up from her knees, but her shoulders stiffened.

She made no move to leave her enclosure.

"Come on out of there. The alligators are all gone."

Aqua whispered something—

"…*n the cage…*"

I paused, perplexed.

"What'd you say?"

"…The world outside the cage is scary… Just take me back to town in here…"

First, frog-related trauma. Now, alligator-related trauma. I guess it was a hard-knock life for a goddess.

10

"Donadonadonaaadooonaaa…"

"Geez, Aqua! Will you quit it with that weird song already? It's bad enough that we're dragging a girl huddled in a cage through the middle of town… And why are you still in there, anyway? We're back. It's safe now. Come out."

"No. This cage is my sanctuary… The outside world is scary. I'm gonna stay in here for now…"

Our horse pulled the cage, where Aqua had apparently decided to take up permanent residence.

People tried their best to look at us without looking at us as we made our way through town, back to the Guild Hall.

Even with a horse-drawn cage (seeing as Aqua was refusing to walk), our progress was slow.

True, one of our number had been severely traumatized—again—but otherwise there was no visible damage to anyone. As eager as we were

to try out our gear and our magic, an uneventful quest was still the best quest.

For us, it was unusual to have an assignment end so…neatly.

Maybe it was my fault for thinking something that pretty much begged for another event flag.

"M-my Lady? My Lady Goddess, it is you, isn't it! Good heavens! What has brought you to this state?!"

A man ran up and grabbed the bars of Aqua's cage. Those bars had withstood the diligent attentions of a swarm of Brutal Alligators, but this man bent them easily, extending a hand to Aqua.

The stranger cast a sidelong glance at me and Megumin, both of us standing there dumbly. He reached out to the equally vacant Aqua, and…

"Aren't you being a little forward with my friend? Exactly who are you? You seem to know Aqua, but she certainly doesn't seem to know you."

Darkness moved in on the man as he made to take Aqua's hand.

She seemed nothing like the girl who'd looked enviously at the caged goddess being assailed by alligators. Now she was a Crusader, a shield, unabashedly protecting her friend.

…What if I could get her to act this way all the time…?

The man gave Darkness a look, sighed, and shook his head. His expression said, *I don't want any trouble, but it seems trouble wants me.* Darkness, usually so reserved, looked openly angered by the man's attitude.

Things were getting tense. I whispered to Aqua, who'd still made no move to get out of the cage:

"Hey, this guy's your buddy, right? He knows you're a goddess and everything. Do something about him!"

For just an instant, Aqua looked at me with a confused but genuine expression.

"...Oh! Goddess! Right, I'm a goddess. So? You want me to handle this situation? Leave it to the goddess..."

She finally wormed her way out of the cage.

...*She didn't* really *forget she's a goddess, right?*

Aqua, now free, gave the stranger a quizzical look.

"Who are you?"

Wait, they don't know each other after all?!

Wait again! Maybe they did.

The guy looked awfully surprised, for his part.

Chances were, Aqua had just forgotten who he was.

"What do you mean, who am I, My Lady?! It is I, Kyouya Mitsurugi! You gave me the magical sword Gram?"

Aqua said nothing, only looked even more confused. I, however, had a sudden thought.

His name sounded like it could have come straight out of an anime, but it was also obviously Japanese. He must have been one of the people who'd run into Aqua before I did.

He seemed very upstanding, and his shock of brown hair made him, actually, pretty handsome. He wore shimmering blue armor that looked very expensive, and a black scabbard hung at his waist.

Two attractive women stood behind him. One carried a spear and seemed to be a warrior; the other wore leather armor with a dagger at her hip.

This Mitsurugi seemed to be about my age. But unlike me, he looked like...well, he looked like the hero of a manga.

"Oh! Yes! I remember you! I'm sorry. I've sent so many people here, it's hard to keep track of them all."

Between us, Mitsurugi and I had finally managed to ignite a spark of recognition in Aqua.

Mitsurugi gave Aqua a slightly strained smile. "I-it's been a long time, Lady Aqua. I'm doing everything I can to complete the mission you gave me. I'm a Sword Master now, Level 37. But...why are you here, milady? And in a cage?" He glanced suspiciously at the rest of us.

I could just see it: Aqua sending this guy off with a song and dance about *You are a hero, chosen for a task...* Blah, blah, blah.

She may have totally forgotten he existed, but I knew all too well the sorts of ridiculous things she'd probably said to him.

Wait a second... Mitsurugi probably thought *I* put Aqua in that cage.

I guess that would be the obvious conclusion to draw from this scene. What were the chances he'd believe me if I told him Aqua had wanted to stay there?

Heck, *I* wouldn't believe me. Who knew such a messed-up goddess even existed?

So I explained to Mitsurugi, as clearly as I could, how Aqua and I had wound up here together, and...

"Ridiculous. Impossible! What were you thinking?! Bringing a goddess to this world! And then putting her in a cage and leaving her in a lake?!"

Mitsurugi, enraged, had me by the collar. In a panic, Aqua tried to intervene.

"N-n-now just a minute! I have a pretty good life here! It doesn't really bother me anymore that he dragged me here, okay? And I can go home if I just defeat the Demon King! Just like our quest today—I was terrified, sure, but in the end we did it and no one got hurt! And the reward is *three hundred thousand*! And they said I could keep all of it!"

Mitsurugi gave Aqua a look of pity.

"Lady Aqua, I don't know what this man did to win you to his side, but your treatment is unjust! All the danger you went through, for a mere three hundred thousand eris? You're a goddess! Is this what you've been reduced to? ...Say, what inn are you staying at?"

I thought we were trying to avoid saying Aqua was a goddess, but

Mitsurugi looked pretty worked up, so I kept my mouth shut. He certainly wasn't keeping his shut, though, saying "goddess" every chance he got.

Some goddess. Mitsurugi clearly didn't know who he was dealing with.

Aqua answered his question hesitantly.

"I-it's not an inn we're all staying at. It's m-more of a…stable."

"What?!" Mitsurugi's grip tightened.

H-hey! That hurts!

Darkness grasped Mitsurugi's other arm.

"I think it's time you let go of my friend. I warn you, grabbing the neck of a man you've just met is *not* the way to make a good first impression."

Usually the only time Darkness talked was when she had something dumb to say, but now she was uncharacteristically angry. I glanced at Megumin and realized she, too, was raising her newly made staff and beginning the chant for Explo— *Waitasecond! Stop that!*

Mitsurugi let me go and looked at Darkness and Megumin with great interest. "A Crusader and an Arch-wizard? And rather fetching ones at that. It seems you've been blessed with fine party members. All the more reason, then, that you should be ashamed of yourself. Forcing Lady Aqua and these fine-looking people to sleep in a stable! If I understand correctly, you're an Adventurer, the lowest class."

Hearing him tell it, even *I* started to think I was pretty lucky. Was that how other people saw me?

I whispered to Aqua:

"Hey, I thought most adventurers slept in stables around here. Isn't that just how it goes? Why is this guy so upset?"

"I gave him a magic sword as an incentive to come here," she said, "so he's been able to take high-level quests from the start. He's probably

never been poor here... Well, that's how it is with most people who have been granted special abilities or equipment."

Unexpectedly, I found myself boiling at Aqua's words. This kid had never had to work for anything here just because he started out with some enchanted sword, and he was lecturing *me*? Me, who'd had to work for everything I had!

Mitsurugi, totally oblivious to my rage, was giving the girls pitying smiles, like he thought that was showing them sympathy.

"Looks like you girls have had a rough time of it. Well, you can stick with me now. I won't let you sleep in any stable, that's for sure. I'll get you the best gear. And the party's balance will be perfect with you! We'll have me, a Sword Master, and my companion, a Warrior, along with you, a Crusader. And on the other hand, my Thief friend here will pair perfectly with this Arch-wizard. And we'll have Lady Aqua, of course. You couldn't ask for a more balanced group!"

Excuse me, I didn't hear my *name anywhere in there.*

Not that I'd want to join this lug's party.

Mitsurugi's attempt to poach my entire group sent my companions into a whispering huddle. He might be a self-centered moron with a messiah complex, but it was still a pretty good offer. It would certainly give Aqua a better chance of achieving her dream of defeating the Demon King. That's what she needed to do to get home, after all. I may have been the one who brought her here, but presumably she could get back no matter who took care of the Big Bad.

I crept up behind them, sure they wouldn't go unmoved by the possibilities.

"Geez, this guy is dangerous—I mean *trouble*. Did you see the way he just assumed we'd come with him? What a narcissist. He's kinda scary."

"I don't understand this feeling. I usually like to *take* the punishment, but for the first time, I want to dish it out instead."

"Can I blast him? Ooh, how I want to put an Explosion right in his coddled face!"

Wow, Mitsurugi, buddy. Rave reviews.

Aqua tugged on my sleeve.

"Come on, Kazuma, let's get back to the Guild. I may have given that kid a sword, but I don't think I want to give him any more of my time."

I was sort of hoping for the opportunity to sock him one before we left, but Aqua was probably right. Discretion would be the better part of valor.

"Well, it looks like all *my* party members are happy where they are. Thanks anyway! If you don't mind, we've got a completed quest to report…"

And, with the horse pulling the cage behind it, we made to leave.

…………

"Could you maybe get out of the way?" I said in annoyance. Mitsurugi was standing directly in front of me.

Some people just didn't know how to take a hint.

"I'm sorry, but Lady Aqua gave me the magic sword Gram, and I cannot allow her to remain in these conditions. You cannot save this world. I will be the one to defeat the Demon King. Lady Aqua *must* come with me." He paused. "You claim that what you chose to bring to this world was Lady Aqua herself, yes?"

"Sure do."

I'd read enough manga to know what was coming next.

He would say—

"In that case, fight me for her. You brought her here like chattel? Well, wager her like it! If I win, relinquish Lady Aqua to me. If you win, I will heed any one thing you ask."

"All right, you're on! Let's go!"

Just as I'd expected.

I'd had enough of this guy. I didn't wait for a countdown or a signal—I flew at him.

I held out the palm of my left hand toward him, pulling out my short sword, sheathe and all, with my right.

Victory goes to the decisive—and all's fair in war!

What was dirtier? A surprise attack? Or a high-level Sword Master with a magic blade challenging a cash-strapped Adventurer to a duel?

I was pretty sure Mitsurugi wasn't expecting me to jump on him even as I answered.

"Wha—? Whoa! Wait—!"

Despite his consternation, though, he was still an experienced adventurer. In a flash, he'd drawn his sword and held it up lengthwise to block me.

As my short sword rang off his blade, I reached out with my left hand and—

"*Steal*!!"

As I shouted, I could feel the weight of a sword fill my hand.

The blade that had been holding back my dagger was suddenly gone from Mitsurugi's hand.

"Huh?" came a chorus of confused voices. I didn't know who they belonged to. Maybe everyone but me.

Mitsurugi had no way to answer my Steal gambit, and with nothing left between us, I slammed my short sword into his head.

"That was a dirty trick! You're a dirty trickster! You rotten, cheating—!"

"You're the worst! You're a low-down, dirty scoundrel! Fight fair!"

Mitsurugi's two companions were busy berating me, but I only listened to them with amusement.

I'd kept my sword sheathed, but it was a pretty heavy piece of equipment, and Mitsurugi had taken a pretty good whack. He was lolling on the ground, his eyes rolled up to the whites.

I declared to his followers:

"So that means I win. He said he'd do any one thing I asked, right? Well, I think I'm gonna *ask* him to give me this sword."

One of the girls said indignantly:

"Wha...?! D-don't be ridiculous! You can't have that! And anyway, only Kyouya can use that sword. Magic blades choose their own masters, and this one has already chosen Kyouya. It won't help you!"

Gee, she sounded so sure of herself. I turned to Aqua.

"Is she right? I can't use this weapon? And here I thought I'd finally gotten a serious item."

"Sorry to say, she's telling the truth. Gram belongs to that beat-up punk over there. Gram's master can equip it to gain superhuman power, a sword that can cut through stone or steel as easily as butter. But if you equipped it, Kazuma, it'd be just a normal sword."

Aww, man...

Well, I worked hard for it. Maybe I ought to take it anyway.

"Okay. Well, when he wakes up, remind him that he started this, so he doesn't get to be upset about it. Come on, Aqua, let's hit the Guild and make our report."

I turned to go, but Mitsurugi's girls raised their weapons.

"H-h-hold it right there!"

"Give back Kyouya's sword. We refuse to acknowledge your victory!"

I stretched out my left hand toward the two girls, palm out.

"Fine. I don't discriminate. I'm perfectly happy to beat up a couple of girls. Don't expect me to hold back. For that matter, remember we're out in public here. And there's no telling *what* I might Steal..."

The two of them looked at my hand and backed up a little, distinctly uneasy. Perhaps they'd realized how much danger they were in.

"Ergh..." I could hear my party say together.

I admit, I was sorry they had to see me like that.

*   *   *

We finally made it back to the Guild Hall, dragging the borrowed cage.

Since we'd decided to give Aqua the whole reward, I let her and the others take care of the report, while I returned the horse and dropped off my "magic" sword somewhere I could retrieve it easily. At last I came to the Guild entrance, where…

"But whyyyy?!"

…I could hear Aqua's petulant wail. She just couldn't be happy until she'd caused a scene.

As I came inside, I saw a tearful Aqua clutching the clerk.

"I told you, I'm not the one who broke your cage! A guy named Mitsurugi did it! Why do *I* have to pay for it?!"

Oh, yeah. I guess he did break open the cage trying to "help" Aqua. Now she was left with the bill. After a bit more struggling, she seemed to accept the fact, took her reward, and trudged back to our table.

"After the price of the cage, the reward is…a hundred thousand eris. They said the cage was made of special metals via an arcane ritual, so it was worth two hundred thousand…"

I couldn't help but feel for her.

She was certainly clear on her feelings about Mitsurugi.

"If I ever see him again, he's gonna get a God Blow to the face—! *And* I'm gonna make him pay me for that cage!"

Aqua sat and began flipping fiercely through the menu, grinding her teeth.

As far as I was concerned, if we ever saw him again, it would be too soon.

And then, as Aqua was still muttering angrily…

"So this is where you've been hiding—Kazuma Satou!"

Well, speak of the devil. Mitsurugi and his two hangers-on were standing in the doorway of the Guild Hall.

Mitsurugi—to whom I had *not* told my full name—strode over to our table and slammed his fist against it.

"Kazuma Satou! A certain young female Thief was only too happy to tell me about you—about how you are a panty-stealing devil! And your predilection for covering girls in slime is known in many quarters. They call you Kazuma the Cur!"

"Wait, wait, wait—who's spreading that stuff around?"

I had a pretty good idea who the Thief was—it was the other rumors I was concerned about.

Some people in some shadowy corners were calling me a "cur"? Telling all kinds of stories about me?!

Mitsurugi approached me, his face serious—but in a single motion, Aqua stood between the two of us.

"...Lady Aqua. I vow to regain my magic blade from this man and defeat the Demon King. So, please... Please... Join my partyyyaaaargh!"

"What?! Kyouya!"

Without a word, Aqua decked Mitsurugi and sent him flying.

Mitsurugi's two companions rushed over to where he lay crumpled on the floor.

He didn't seem to understand why Aqua had punched him. Aqua, for her part, briskly walked up to him and grabbed him by the collar.

"They charged *me* for that cage you ruined! You had better pay me back! Three hundred grand! Did you know that cage was made of special metals and—and arcane rituals? It was expensive! Now pay up!"

Hadn't she said it was worth two hundred thousand?

Mitsurugi—nursing a quickly forming bruise, sitting on his butt after having been punched, and overawed by Aqua's onslaught—politely got out his wallet and gave her the money.

Aqua took the cash and then opened a menu, looking quite pleased with herself.

Mitsurugi had collected himself by that point. Clearly frustrated with Aqua, who was happily holding the menu in one hand and gesturing for a waiter with the other, he said to me in a voice heavy with regret:

"Even if your methods were dishonorable, a loss is a loss. And I said I would give you anything you asked, so I know what I am about to say may seem outrageous…but…I beg you! Will you not return my magic sword? It is of no special use to you. If you wield it, it will cut no better, strike no harder, than any weapon here… What do you say? If you want a sword, I'll buy you the best one in the shop. So will you not give back my precious Gram?"

He was right. That *was* outrageous.

After all, as useless as she may be, Aqua was what I'd chosen to bring with me to this world. In other words, she was to me what the magic sword was to him. (Was she actually worth as much as a magic sword? Don't ask.)

"What, you think it *wouldn't* have been inexcusable to wager me against some non-magic sword? Or are you trying to say I'm worth only as much as the most expensive sword here? Some honor! What were you even thinking, asking someone to wager a goddess?! I'm tired of looking at you. Shoo! Shoo!"

Mitsurugi paled as Aqua waved the menu at him dismissively.

Well, I could hardly blame her for being upset—he was the one who'd come up with the whole idea of a bet to begin with.

"L-L-Lady Aqua, wait! By no means do I undervalue you—!"

Mitsurugi was distracted in his panic by Megumin, who gave a sharp tug on his sleeve.

"Huh? Ahem—can I help you, little girl…?"

Megumin pointed at me.

Specifically, at my waist.

"First, note that he is no longer wearing the magic sword."

Noticing for the first time that the sword wasn't at my hip, Mitsurugi almost choked.

"K-Kazuma Satou! Where is Gram? What have you done with my sword?!"

He clung to me, sweat running down his face. I had two words for him:

"Sold it."

"Damn it allllll!"

Mitsurugi dashed from the Guild Hall, weeping.

"Sheesh, what's with him, anyway?" It was shortly after Mitsurugi had fled the hall. Darkness approached Aqua, the room's curiosity aroused by the commotion. "And...he keeps calling you a goddess, Aqua. What does he mean by that?"

Well, he said it so many times, I guess someone was bound to ask.

We'd made it this far, though. Maybe it was time to come clean with Megumin and Darkness.

I looked at Aqua, and she nodded as if she understood. Then she turned to Darkness and Megumin with an uncharacteristically serious expression. Picking up on Aqua's attitude, the two of them listened just as gravely.

"I've been keeping this to myself, but I can tell you two. I am Aqua—the water deity worshipped by the Axis Church. It's true! I—even I—am the goddess Aqua!"

"What was this, a dream you had?" they responded together.

"No, it wasn't! Why did you say that in unison, anyway?"

I guess that's about what you could expect...

That was when it happened.

"*Urgent! Urgent!* All adventurers, please equip your weapons and items and prepare for battle at the town gate!"

The familiar sound of an emergency announcement echoed through the streets.

"Again? Sure seems like we've had a lot of those lately."

Did we *have* to go?

I guess we did. It was just such a pain, right after dealing with Mitsurugi and all...

I dragged myself up from the table.

*   *   *

"*Urgent! Urgent!* All adventurers, please equip your weapons and items and prepare for battle at the town gate! ...Will Adventurer Kazuma Satou and his party in particular please hurry?"

"...*What?*"

Aww, man...what now?

Chapter 4

May There Be an End to This Useless Battle!

1

I rushed to the main square.

Megumin, Aqua, and I were all lightly armored and were able to get there quickly; Darkness, with her heavy equipment, brought up the rear.

"I knew it. *Him* again."

A number of adventurers had already gathered by the time we arrived.

A crowd of novices carefully kept their distance from the gate proper, where *he* stood.

That's right—the Demon King's general. The Dullahan.

I noticed how pale the other adventurers looked, but it wasn't until I glanced behind the Dullahan that I understood.

This time, he wasn't alone.

A horde of monsters—Knights in decaying armor—backed him up. Look too hard at what was inside their armor, and you'd probably lose your lunch or be permanently traumatized… In between the battered plates and behind the creaking visors, you could catch glimpses of rotting corpses.

It didn't take an adventurer to tell that these were the undead.

When the Dullahan spied Megumin and me, he burst out:

"Why haven't you come to my castle, you miscreants?!"

I stepped out in front of Megumin, covering her with my body, and said:

"Umm… Why should we? And who's a miscreant? We haven't set off one explosion since you asked us to stop. Why're you so upset?"

At that, the Dullahan raised the object in his left hand and *almost* flung it to the ground, before he remembered that it was his own head. He hurriedly pulled it back next to him.

"You haven't set off a single explosion, have you? Not one magical blast? Ridiculous! Your insane Crimson friend has come by every single day!"

"Huh?"

I looked at Megumin.

She looked away.

"You went to his castle? I told you not to go, and you still went?!"

"O-o-o-o-o-owww! That hurts! D-do not misunderstand, Kazuma— let me explain! I used to be able to get by just setting off an explosion in an empty field. B-but now that I have tasted the joy of exploding a castle, I need to cast my spell on something huge and hard…!"

"I know what it means when you get all fidgety! And anyway, you can't move after you cast Explosion. Which means…you must have had an accomplice. Now, who was it…?"

Aqua saw me tugging on Megumin's cheek and suddenly averted her eyes.

I took a deep breath.

"Was it *youuuu*?!"

"Yaaaah! We just wanted to get him back for keeping us from finding any good quests! *He's* the reason I spend every day being screamed at by the shopkeeper!"

Excuse me, but I think that's because you do terrible work.

As I caught a fleeing Aqua by the back of her collar, the Dullahan continued speaking:

"What angers me most is not that you insist on your puny pyrotechnics—but that you have no desire to help your friend! Before

I was unjustly put to death and transformed by my anger into the monster you see before you, I was a Knight. And as a Knight, I tell you—to abandon that Crusader, who selflessly shielded you from my curse with her own body, trading her life for yours, the very image of Knighthood…"

At that moment, Darkness finally ran up to my side, her heavy armor clattering as she moved.

Her face was red from the Dullahan's praises. Their eyes met.

"H…hey."

Darkness waved, almost apologetically, at the Dullahan.

"…Wh…whaaaaa…?!"

The Dullahan screeched.

His expression was hidden behind his helmet, but I assumed his face showed plain shock.

"Aww, what is it? Are you surprised to see Darkness alive and well? Even though it's been more than a week? Were you waiting for us in your little castle this whole time? Never knowing that I broke the curse on Darkness, like, five minutes after you left? Pffft! That's rich! That's too much!"

Aqua pointed at the Dullahan, gripped by gales of laughter.

I didn't need to see the Dullahan's face—his shoulders were trembling. He was hopping mad.

But Aqua *had* broken the curse, after all, and why should we wander right into his trap for no reason?

"Do you understand who you're dealing with, you impudent knave? If I wanted to, I could wipe out every adventurer in this town, put all its inhabitants to the sword! Don't think I'll look the other way forever! My immortal body knows no fatigue. You would be as chicks before the wolf—you could not so much as touch me!"

Aqua's taunting had obviously pushed the Dullahan to the breaking point; the anger veritably rolled off him.

Before he could make a move, though, Aqua thrust out her right hand and shouted: "*You* won't look the other way?! What about me?

You've got some nerve, causing all this trouble! Now, go back where you came from, monster—*Turn Undead*!!"

A white light flew from Aqua's hand.

The Dullahan, though, made no move to escape—just watched Aqua as though her magic meant nothing to him.

I guess that's the kind of confidence you have when you're one of the Demon King's generals.

The white light emanating from Aqua began to surround the Dullahan…

"Did you suppose the servants of the Demon King went into battle without taking measures against Priests? You fool! Not only I but every Undead Knight with me is resistant to holy magic by the grace of His Majesty, the Devil Kiiii—aaaggh!"

Wherever the light touched him, black smoke began to rise.

But even though he was smoking and shaking, his confidence shattered, the Dullahan held his ground.

"I don't understand, Kazuma!" Aqua cried. "It's not working!"

I don't know. I would've said it seemed to be working pretty well, what with the tortured scream and all.

"Heh-heh-heh-heh-heh! This is why you shouldn't interrupt, girl. I am Beldia—Dullahan and general of the Demon King! His Majesty specially blessed my armor, and when combined with my own power, it makes me impervious to your silly Turn Undead! …Impervious, all right? Say, Priest, what level are you, anyway? Are you really a beginner? This *is* the starter town, isn't it?"

He tilted the hand holding his head just a bit. I guess it was supposed to look inquisitive.

"…Well, never mind. I came here to investigate when our soothsayer babbled something about a great light that fell near this town… But it's too much trouble. We'd do better just to wipe this place off the map."

Seriously? I'd heard childhood bullies say less awful things. Still clutching his head in his left hand, Beldia raised his right hand high.

"Hmph! I need not even bother myself with you lot. Minions! Rain hell upon these disrespectful dogs!"

"Hey! He's running scared because Aqua's magic actually worked on him! He's gonna get to safety and leave his underlings to fight us!"

"Th-th-that's not true at all! This was my plan from the start! H-how dare you insinuate that a general of the Demon King would act out of cowardice?! You don't get to go straight to the boss battle. First you fight the minions, then you fight the boss! That's how things have worked since time immemori—"

"*Sacred Turn Undead*!!"

"Eyyyyaaarrrghh!" Beldia's rant turned into a scream as Aqua's magic hit him.

A circle formed at his feet, and a white light lanced up from it into the sky.

Smoke began to billow from Beldia; he threw himself to the ground and began to roll around as though his armor were on fire.

"Wh-what do we do, Kazuma?! I knew something was weird! My magic doesn't work at all on him!"

I really think "eyargh!" means it's working.

Then again, Turn Undead usually worked in one go.

It might mean…

"Wh-why, you—! Let me finish for once! Very well—minions!"

Still smoking here and there, Beldia raised his right hand.

"Destroy this town. And everyone in it!"

He brought down his hand.

2

Undead Knights.

They were a top class of zombie, and though their armor might not have looked like much, they wore it well. These monsters were more than enough to terrorize novice adventurers.

"Oh no! A Priest! Call a Priest!"

"Somebody go to the Eris Church and get all the holy water you can!"

The adventurers' panicked cries rang out as the Undead Knights advanced into the city.

Adventurers lined up to face the monsters.

And Beldia watched it all, laughing…

"Ah-ha-ha-ha-ha! I shall enjoy listening to your cries of despair! Your…cries—"

A shout from the crowd had interrupted his merriment.

"Yiiiikes! Why are you all coming after me?! I'm a goddess! My life isn't supposed to be this hard!"

"Aww, not fair! My life *isn't* hard! Why not attack me?!"

That would be Aqua, shouting some most un-goddess-like things, and Darkness, exclaiming in envy.

The Knights hadn't moved toward the townspeople but, for some reason, were heading relentlessly for Aqua.

"N-no, you fools! Don't get distracted by one Priest! There are other adventurers right there, you know! Townspeople! Let's get a bloodbath going here!" Beldia sounded more than a little dismayed.

Maybe his mindless undead minions were naturally drawn to Aqua, who was a goddess and could bring them salvation.

It was just a theory. But it was also irrelevant. The point was, now was our chance!

"Hey, Megumin! Think you can land an explosion right in the middle of those Undead Knights?"

"What?! But we are in town—think of the collateral damage!"

Then it happened.

"Sir Kazumaaaa! Great Kazumaaaa!"

Aqua was dashing toward me, a horde of Undead Knights right behind her.

Wha—?!

"You idiot! Stop! Stay back! If you turn around, I'll treat you to dinner tonight!"

"*I'll* treat *you*—just do something about these undead! They're not normal! My Turn Undead skill doesn't make them disappear!"

Dammit. Was this what Beldia had meant by the grace of the Demon King?

No…wait. Wait just a second.

"Megumin! Get outside the gate and start chanting!"

"What? Y-yes, sir!"

With that, I ran for the gate myself, Aqua and the monsters hot on my heels. I made sure to run right by the few Undead Knights who were fighting other adventurers, hoping to add as many as possible to our collection…

Then…

"Kazuma, pleeeease! The Knights? The undead ones? They're *right behind me*!"

I looked back and saw a massive army of Beldia's servants following us.

Aqua and I passed the town gate. Then the Knights went through. And then…

"Megumin, now!"

At my signal, Megumin held up her staff, red eyes flashing.

"A better moment I could not have dreamed! My thanks, Kazuma, my deepest thanks! …My name is Megumin! First among the spell-casters of the Crimson Magic Clan! Master of explosive magics! O Beldia, general of the Demon King, behold my power! *Explosion*!!"

The blast from Megumin's beloved spell landed smack in the center of the crowd of zombies.

3

The magical blast left a vast crater immediately outside the town gate. There was no sign of any of the Undead Knights.

Everyone was struck dumb by the power of the spell.

"Heh-heh-heh," came Megumin's triumphant voice. "It seems the sight of my power has silenced you all… Ha-ha-ha… If I may say so, that was tremendously…*satisfying*…"

"Need a ride?"

"Y-yes, please."

Nearby, Megumin was collapsed face-first on the ground.

I hefted her onto my back.

"Ptooie! Yuck! It's like I've got sand in my mouth…"

Aqua had been closest to the Knights. Now she walked along spitting little particles out of her mouth. The force of the blast had kicked up plenty of dirt.

Through the smoke that was still billowing out of the crater, we could hear the adventurers in the town give a cheer.

"Yahoo! Way to go, you crazy kid!"

"That crazy Crimson Magic Clan girl did it!"

"She's as crazy as her name is weird, but she sure comes through when it counts! You can call me a fan!"

I could feel Megumin squirming at the town's approbation.

"Excuse me. Could you please carry me over that way? I wish to dispatch those people with an explosion."

"You're all out of spells for today. Anyway, you did a really good job. You should be proud of yourself. Stick out your chest and enjoy a break… You've earned it."

At that, Megumin settled against me, mollified.

Something soft pressed against my back…

Something…soft…?

I guess she was sticking out her chest like I'd suggested, but you could hardly tell.

…*Well, that's jailbait for you, I guess.*

"Crimson Magic Clan members have extremely high Intelligence," Megumin said suddenly from behind me. "Shall I guess what you are thinking now, Kazuma?"

"I was just thinking, I didn't know you were so svelte under all that armor."

I was patronizing her, and she knew it. For a second, I thought she was going to choke me.

But Beldia was there, at the town gate, looking at us.

More precisely, looking at Megumin, riding on my back.

Gradually, his shoulders began to tremble.

We had destroyed all his undead servants. It was only natural that he'd be mad.

…Or not.

"Bwa-ha-ha-ha-ha! Excellent! Wonderful! I never imagined this starter town might be home to someone who could actually defeat all my underlings! Then…I shall now keep my promise!"

…Wait a second.

Hold it right there—!

"I shall face you in battle myself!"

With that, Beldia drew a massive sword and leaped at us.

4

Faster than Beldia could reach us, several adventurers moved to defend us, surrounding him with weapons in hand.

Beldia took in the situation and then, head in one hand and blade in the other, shrugged easily.

"Hmm? I'm most interested in *them*, but… Heh-heh. I see. Should one of you perchance topple me, no doubt there will be a significant reward to be had. Very well! You adventurers dream of getting rich quick? Well, come and earn it!"

The adventurers surrounding him grew excited at the Dullahan's mention of a quick buck.

One guy, a warrior if I had to guess, called out to those around him: "I don't care how strong he is, he ain't got eyes in the back of his head! Circle up, everyone, and we'll all hit him at once!"

Welp. What a death flag.

"Hey!" I shouted to the cannon fodder. "This is the Demon King's general we're talking about here! You think he'll fall for a trick like that?"

Even as I spoke, I started to raise my own sword to help them…

…and stopped. *Think!* I'm pretty much the weakest possible character. If I took a swing at him, what would happen?

The important thing now was to get Megumin somewhere safe…

And then what?

Megumin was out of MP. Aqua's magic wasn't doing the trick.

Maybe the best plan would be for all of us to just run like hell.

As I was having that thought, the warrior was moving to attack Beldia in earnest.

"I don't have to kill him! I just have to buy us some time! The town's ace must have heard the urgent announcement—he'll be coming! If we can hold out till he gets here, that'll be it—general of the Demon King or no! Come on, everyone, he must have a blind spot! Let's come from everywhere at once!"

Faced with the bellowing warrior, Beldia took his head in his hand and…tossed it into the air?

The town's ace?

Who could that be? Presumably some famous, powerful adventurer…

Beldia's head floated above the fray, drifting until it faced straight down toward the ground.

I saw it and froze.

So did everyone else—everyone watching seemed to have realized at the same time.

"Stop! Stay ba—"

We called out, tried to stop the nameless adventurers.

Beldia answered the oncoming circle of fighters as if he could see everywhere at once.

"Huh?" I heard an adventurer gasp as he was cut down.

I wondered who he was.

Having stopped all his attackers, Beldia changed his grip on his sword from one hand to two...

...and in the blink of an eye, he cut down all the adventurers who'd come at him.

People who'd been alive seconds before were suddenly gone, blank-eyed and limp.

It was outrageous. It was unbearable. It was a reminder that this world was all too real.

The sound of men crumpling.

Beldia listened gleefully, then raised one hand. Its outstretched palm caught his head neatly.

It seemed as if he'd hardly broken a sweat murdering an entire crowd of adventurers.

"Who's next?" he said easily.

The remaining adventurers quailed at the words.

But one girl's voice rang out:

"Y-you big bully! Just wait till Mitsurugi gets here! He'll take you out in one hit!"

.........What?

My heart almost stopped.

Mitsurugi? The guy whose magic sword I'd taken and then sold? *That* Mitsurugi?

"Right!" another voice cried. "Just hold on! When that boy and his magic blade get here, not even the Demon King's general will be able to—"

"Beldia, was it? We may be a starter town, but we've got a few powerful friends of our own!"

Oh crap. Oh *crap*.

The only person in this town besides Mitsurugi who had a chance against Beldia was Aqua, and she was ignoring the Dullahan completely. For some reason, she was scurrying from one of the fallen adventurers to the next, placing her hands on the bodies.

Maybe she was doing what a goddess does, trying to offer them a prayer on their way into the afterlife.

Beldia stood lazily, observing his handiwork. Heavily armored adventurers lay dead at his feet, and now no one would challenge him…

"Oh-ho? Do you seek to be my next victim?"

Beldia held his head in his left hand, his great sword in his right.

He held the head out on his palm to inspect Darkness, who'd moved to cover Megumin and me.

With the two of us behind her and her sword at the ready, Darkness was not the weird pervert who caused me so much trouble. She was a Crusader I would be proud to be seen with anywhere.

Beldia had seen just how powerful Aqua and Megumin were. He probably assumed Darkness had something up her sleeve, too.

He stood across from her, not moving.

Darkness's white armor shone in the sunlight, in stark contrast to Beldia's pitch-black plate.

The adventurers who'd attacked him earlier had all been armored, too. But the Demon King's general had cut through their armor like paper. Darkness prided herself on being tougher than anyone—but would it be enough to withstand his attacks?

Darkness seemed to understand that I was fighting with myself about whether to stop her—she said bravely to me:

"Don't worry, Kazuma. I can take a hit better than anyone. And skills affect weapons and armor as well. No denying Beldia has an excellent sword. But a sword alone isn't enough to cut through armor the way he did. It looks to me like Beldia's specialized in attack skills. So we'll just have to see which is better. His attack…or my defense!"

Actually, she seemed unusually prepared to attack, herself.

"Give it up! It's not just attack—he has serious Evasion, too. Did you see how he dodged all those opponents? You can't hit a target that's standing still! What are you gonna do?"

Darkness's gaze didn't waver from Beldia as I spoke.

"As a paladin…as one whose vocation is to protect…there is one thing on which I will never bend. Let me do this."

I had no idea what she was talking about—but I guess even Darkness had her own reason to keep fighting.

As I stood there, silent, Darkness hefted her great sword and lunged at Beldia.

"Oh-ho! A feisty one! I was once a knight—what better opponent could I have than a paladin? Have at you, then!" And Beldia prepared to meet her.

He looked at the huge blade Darkness held and dropped into a low, evasive stance, as if afraid to take a blow from her sword.

Darkness leaned in with the blade as if she was going to slam into him with her entire body weight…

…and rammed her sword into the ground a few centimeters from Beldia. Maybe she'd misjudged the distance?

"…Huh?" Beldia said flatly.

He stared in surprise at Darkness. All the other adventurers in the square wore the same expression.

…*Geez! Can't she even hit someone standing still?!*

She might have been my party member, but I mean—gosh. I'd heard of amateurs who swung their swords so recklessly, they ended up chopping off their own foot. But this?

Darkness, for her part, didn't seem the least bit chagrined, but simply took a step forward and reset her stance, holding out the sword to one side.

Her cheeks were the tiniest bit red, betraying a hint of embarrassment at missing her mark after all that buildup.

Maybe she had the right angle—because Beldia settled even deeper into his stance, ready to evade.

"Such a disappointment. Enough... Now...," he said, sounding almost bored. Then he casually let loose a single strike at Darkness, down and across from shoulder to hip.

"Now, then...who's...next? What?"

No doubt he assumed he'd taken her out. But Beldia's sword simply dragged along Darkness's armor. The only results were a scratch and an earsplitting noise.

Darkness stepped back, putting some distance between them.

"Aww, man! M-my brand-new armor...!" She groaned as she looked at the huge gouge, then glared at Beldia.

It was a deep cut, but not deep enough to reach Darkness underneath the armor.

In other words...

"Wh-what are you?! You take my blow and are not cloven... That armor must be a master's work. And yet...even if it was, still... Your Arch-priest, your explosive Arch-wizard... The lot of you are..."

While Beldia was busy muttering to himself, I slipped in among the other adventurers. I passed Megumin to one of them, then turned and shouted: "Darkness! You can withstand his attacks! I'm coming—leave the offense to me!"

Darkness nodded, not looking away from Beldia. "All right. But I have a request—help me get one blow against this monster!"

I shouted back that I understood. Then I turned to the nearby adventurers. "All spell-casters!"

My words seemed to bring everyone back to themselves. Everyone who knew any spells began furiously preparing their magic. Everyone who didn't started looking for something they could help with.

We were in a fight with one of the Demon King's generals, here.

A major enemy had shown up at our doorstep. There was no reason we should let him go home unscathed.

But Beldia had planted his sword in the ground and was pointing his empty right hand at one chanting spell-caster after another.

"In one week's time! All of you! Shall die!!"

He placed his death curse on all the mages at once. And one by one, cowed by the realization that they were going to die, each of them stopped chanting.

Other spell-casters who'd been preparing to get in on the fight took one look at their cursed colleagues and quietly refrained from casting any spells.

Stinking Dullahan! That was a dirty trick!

"Now, how about a real test?"

As Beldia shouted, he flung his head up in the air again.

…*I wonder if we could get an archer to shoot down that head?*

I was still working my way through that thought when Beldia grabbed his sword with both hands and charged at Darkness.

His helmet was looking down at the ground, just like the last time. It must have let him see the entire battlefield—air reconnaissance, so to speak.

It eliminated his blind spots, made it easy to guess where his opponents would dodge.

From behind me, Megumin gave an anguished cry.

"K-Kazuma! Darkness is…!"

I looked around the square. Almost every adventurer in town was there.

Some of them I knew. There was the person who'd taught me the weaknesses of some monsters.

One girl had drawn a bow but was holding back the shot, afraid she might hit Darkness instead of Beldia. She was the one who'd introduced me to Neroid.

The older guy who'd teased me at the Guild Hall for not drinking alcohol. He held a spear and was trying to circle around behind Beldia.

If Darkness fell, Beldia really might kill all these people. Just on a whim.

Darkness… Darkness herself seemed to know it. She'd turned the flat of her huge blade outward, toward the oncoming foe. She stood without moving, like a shield.

Hit me, her stance seemed to say. *Except on my head. I'm not wearing a helmet.*

"I like the lively ones!" Beldia cried. "How about *this*, then?!" He grasped his sword in both hands and unleashed blow after blow, more than any mortal could have made.

One, two, three, four…!

Soon it was ten strikes, then more. Each one made a grating sound of metal on metal and left a mark on Darkness's armor.

Any one of those strikes would have cut down an average adventurer. But Darkness weathered them all without flinching.

A few strands of her golden hair, caught by the blade, danced into the air.

Beldia let up for a moment to catch his head as it came tumbling back out of the sky. He made an appreciative noise at Darkness's durability, then gave a one-handed swing of his sword.

The magic-users stood, watching Darkness endure.

They were pale from shock…

…but as if finally resolved, they began to chant again.

I felt something warm dribble down my cheek.

I wiped at it with my hand. It was…

"Darkness, you're hurt! Stand down—you've done enough! We'll all scatter, come up with a new plan!"

I could see blood dripping from her cheeks, from the gouges in her armor.

In spite of my urging, though, she didn't back down.

"A Crusader will never abandon her place when there are lives at stake!" she said. "That alone is absolute. A-and—!"

She sure knew how to talk a good game. Her cheeks grew redder and redder as she tried to play it up, too...

"A-and this Dullahan kn-knows what he's doing! He's planning to chip away at my armor until there's only one piece left—he's going to humiliate me by leaving me here—not even totally exposed—he'll leave me just covered enough to inflame the imaginations of all and sundry...!"

"Say what?"

Beldia froze for an instant at Darkness's outrageous suggestion. As I quietly started to prepare some magic, I also began to abuse our resident pervert. I guess a degenerate leopard couldn't change its spots, even at a time like this.

"Hey, ever heard of choosing a time and place more carefully? You're the perviest perv who ever perved!"

Darkness began to tremble a little at my words.

"Erk...! K-Kazuma! Speak for yourself! I have my hands full here being beaten up in public by a Dullahan! If you start abusing me, too...! A-are you and this Dullahan secretly in league together?!"

"Whaaat?!"

"As if, you perv! *Create Water!*"

At my shout, water appeared over the combatants' heads. It came down as fast as if I'd emptied a bucket over them.

Darkness was soaked from head to toe. And Beldia...Beldia was trying desperately to avoid the water.

...?

*   *   *

What's he so worried about?

Darkness, dripping, turned red and muttered, "An ambush... N-not bad, Kazuma, not bad at all. But you really should learn to pick your moment..."

"Th-this isn't some sick game, you nut! It's *this*! *Freeze*!"

I intoned some basic magic to freeze water. By itself, it didn't do much. But on wet ground...

Beldia gave a start. "Oh-ho! You've frozen my feet as a little obstacle, have you? I see you think Evasion is my only strength. How wrong you are!"

I jumped toward the ice-legged Dullahan, ready to deploy my real skill.

That's right. The one I'd used on Mitsurugi. My most powerful weapon!

"I just needed to slow you down! I'll have your sword now, Dullahan—*Steal*!"

I slammed into him with my skill, my random-item-grabbing Steal ability.

Spells and skills were ubiquitous in this world. They drew on MP, which everyone had, rather than HP.

Aqua once told me that there used to be lots of people on Earth, too, who could use magic. We'd just forgotten how.

And by using more MP, you could increase the power of your skills or spells, as well as their success rate.

I'd managed to literally freeze Beldia in place. I had him right where I wanted him, a sitting duck for my ultimate ability...!

"Not bad, boy. No doubt you were quite sure it would work. But I *am* the Demon King's general. Remember the difference in our levels. If you were more powerful or I less, I might have been in trouble. But as it is..."

...My skill had had no effect on Beldia at all.

*   *   *

He pointed at me.

…Well, this was no good. I guess I should've known Steal wouldn't work on one of the Demon King's own generals.

Before Beldia could curse me, though, there was a shout.

"Hands off my friend!"

Darkness had none of her usual cool; her anger was obvious. As she shouted, she threw aside her huge sword, a weapon she couldn't hit anything with anyway, and launched herself at Beldia in a massive body slam.

Beldia might have been stuck to the ground, but he still dodged her easily, and with time to spare, he adjusted his grip on his sword.

Darkness had thrown away her sword to try that body blow.

She had nothing to defend herself with.

Before I knew it, I was shouting.

"Thieves, help me! Maybe it's a one-in-ten-thousand chance, but if even one of us can get that sword away from him, we win! Everyone who can use Steal, come with me!"

Maybe there was *someone* out there with a higher level or better Luck than mine.

Thieves appeared at my side one after another, silently, thanks to their Ambush skills.

"*Steal*!" we exclaimed together.

But none of our attempts did anything.

Beldia didn't even seem to notice us. Instead, he was taking a stance, facing the defenseless Darkness… And then he tossed his head up in the air again.

"Oh, no!"

A collective groan went up from the gathered adventurers.

We all knew the head in the air was the prelude to his crushing two-handed rain of blows.

"…Hrk…!"

Darkness gave a small squeak.

No, no, no, no, no!

What was I supposed to *do*?!

I didn't have any special abilities. No hidden talents.

There was nothing I could show off or be proud of. And certainly no skills that would help us now.

All I had was better-than-average Luck.

And a knowledge of video games built up over a lifetime.

It was all those days I'd spent playing games instead of doing anything productive that had brought me here. I'd been thrilled to find myself in a real fantasy world. Was I going to have to stand by helplessly and watch it all be destroyed?

"Darkness! Kazuma, Darkness is—!"

I could hear Megumin shouting from behind me.

Think! Think back to your RPGs. You're up against a Dullahan. What's his weakness?

If I'd ever had what you could call a specialty, it was that in PVP matches online, I could immediately pick out which attack or strategy would annoy my opponent most.

Look at him. Observe him.

…Why did he try to run away from the water I made?

…

Running water.

High Undead and vampires were weak to it.

What about Dullahans?

"I have enjoyed this, Crusader! As a former knight, I am grateful to the Dark Gods and the Demon King that I was able to try myself against you! And now…"

He made to attack her in earnest…

"*Create Water*!!"

"?!"

Beldia stopped where he was, coming up short of attacking Darkness.

He didn't make even a single sword stroke, only caught his head as it came down.

"Kazuma, I… I'm trying to have a serious battle here…"

Darkness was even wetter than before, and she did not look happy about it.

Under other circumstances, I might have apologized. Not now.

Instead, I bellowed:

"Waaaaterrrrr!"

5

"*Create Water*! *Create Water*! *Create Water*!!"

"Hrrgh! Yargh!"

At my direction, spell-casters all over the square began chanting.

Even with buckets of water spilling over his head, Beldia kept dodging our downpours.

Damn! We'd finally figured out his weakness, but we couldn't hit him!

I could see the other magic-users growing fatigued. At this rate, we'd all run out of MP before we ever landed a drop on Beldia.

That was when I heard it.

"Hey, what's going on here? Why are you all having a water fight with the Demon King's general? Here I am actually working for once, and I come back to find you playing games? What kind of idiot are you, Kazuma?"

Sometimes I could just smack her.

Aqua had reappeared from wherever she'd gone and was now trotting through the crowd with her ridiculous complaining as the rest of us desperately cast water magic.

"Water—! His weakness is water! You may just barely qualify at the very bottom of the scale, but you *are* a water goddess, aren't you? A *goddess*, right? Even if you're a dumb one? Well, how about some damn water already?!"

"You know, you are in for some divine retribution one of these days, you ingrate! I'm not just barely qualified or at the very bottom of the scale or dumb or anything—I'm a bona fide celestial being! Water? You want water? Ha! I could make a flood that would put your little dribbles to shame! But you have to apologize for calling me all those mean things!"

Could she really do that?

Well, why wasn't she doing it already?!

"I'll apologize a million times if you want—later! If you've got a flood in you, then let it out, you useless goddess!"

"Waaaaah! How can you call me a useless goddess? Just you watch! I'll show you what a goddess is good for!"

I'd put out the bait, and she'd swallowed it.

Aqua took a step forward.

A mist began to swirl around her.

…Huh?

"You poor fools! You think your little cloudbursts could ever—Hmm?"

Beldia stopped dead when he saw Aqua.

That's a Demon King general for you: I guess he could tell that whatever Aqua was doing was bad news.

Then again, all the spell-casters nearby were warily looking at her, too.

Aqua was muttering to herself, oblivious to the looks of everyone around her.

"O my followers in this world…"

The mist around her began to bead into droplets of water.

I could feel each of them take in a bit of magic.

"...Aqua, goddess of water, commands you..."

...I had a bad feeling about this. Something about the way the air all around us seemed to tremble.

It reminded me of the feeling in the air just before Megumin let off an explosion.

Meaning Aqua had something just as powerful, and just as dangerous, up her sleeve...!

Beldia obviously had the same sense of foreboding I did.

Without a moment's hesitation, he turned his back on Aqua and began to run.

...But he stopped when he saw Darkness in front of him.

Aqua brought her hands together.

"*Sacred Create Water*!!"

And then the floodgates opened.

6

When Aqua said *flood*, she wasn't kidding.

"N-no! Wait!"

"Yaaagh! W-waaaterrrr!"

The waves crashed down on not just Beldia, but Darkness and the other adventurers nearby. They reached Megumin and me and even Aqua, fresh off her chant.

"Hrgh! Grg—! I-I'm drowning—!"

"Megumin! Megumiiin! Grab on to me! You'll get washed away!"

Everyone was getting caught in the deluge.

The waves crashed down in front of the town gate with a massive spray, then began to run into Axel.

When the water finally receded, the ground was covered with top-pled adventurers. And…

"Wh—pfft—what were you fools thinking?! Y-you idiots! You—you foolish idiots!"

…there was Beldia, unsteadily hefting himself up from the ground.

Frankly, I pretty much agreed with him. But now wasn't the time.

This was our chance, our best—

"This is our chance! Our best shot at taking him down! My amazing display of magical prowess has weakened him—! Now go, Kazuma! Finish him off! Quick! Go already!"

Why, that stinking useless…

I made a mental note to Steal her so much, she'd break down crying from shame in front of everybody. But that would come later. For now, I raised my hand toward Beldia…

"Your weapon's mine, for real this time. Take *this*!"

"Do your worst! Even in my weakened state, I would hardly succumb to some amateur's Steal technique!"

As he shouted at me, he lobbed his head into the air one more time, gripping his great sword with both hands and projecting the most intimidating picture he could manage.

He was a general of the Demon King to the last. We'd hit him right in his weak spot, and somehow I was the one whose knees were trembling.

He might have been a general. He was also my target.

"*Steal*!!"

I put every ounce of strength into my technique.

Instantly, I felt something hard and cold; a solid weight filled my hands.

I did it! I thought. And of course, thinking that would set off another event flag.

"Ohhh…"

The adventurers around me gave a collective despairing moan.

I looked at Beldia. He was still holding his sword.

I braced myself for his brutal cut attack…

                    *   *   *

…but it never came. He just stood there.

………?

Silence fell over the befuddled crowd.

Then, we heard a voice, small and afraid.

"U-uhm…"

It was *Beldia*'s voice. And it was trembling.

"Could I… Could I have my head back, please…?"

The voice was coming from the weight in my hands.

……………

"Hey, everyone!" I said. "Ever heard of soccer? It's a game where you move the ball using only your *feet*!"

I gave Beldia's head a kick toward the crowd of adventurers.

"Yaaargh! H-hey, stop that!"

The tumbling head immediately became nothing more than a toy for the men and women who'd been cowed by it moments before.

"Haaa-ha-ha-ha! I like this game!"

"Hey, over here! Pass it to me!"

"Yaaagh! Stoppit! That hurts! Stop!"

The Dullahan's body, thoroughly blind, stood stupefied with the sword in its hands.

"Hey, Darkness! You said you wanted a shot at him, right?"

I picked up the sword she'd dropped and took it over to where Darkness stood sopping wet, breathing hard and dripping blood from a variety of wounds. She raised the blade and took a stance facing Beldia's body.

I gestured to Aqua to join us.

She came over, still wringing out her feather mantle.

Darkness raised her sword high—

"This! Is for all those I cared for whom you killed! Only one blow—for them all!"

She brought it down hard.

"Graaaaghh!"

I could hear Beldia's muffled scream from inside the crowd of newly minted soccer players.

Darkness might not be very precise, but she was very strong. Beldia's black chest plate cracked down the middle.

I recalled Beldia saying something about that armor being specially blessed by the Demon King.

"All right, Aqua. You take care of the rest."

"You got it!"

Beldia's armor was shattered; the flood had left him weak. Aqua stretched out her hand.

"*Sacred Turn Undead*!"

"W-waiiiii—eyaaarrrrgghhh!"

We heard Beldia's head bellow, over by some adventurer's foot.

This time, it worked.

A white light enveloped Beldia's body, and gradually the light and the body faded and vanished.

The head went with it, raising a groan from the adventurers, who'd apparently been having fun learning to play soccer.

That was how we got rid of one of the Demon King's generals. But we never did learn why he'd come to the area…

7

The triumphant shouts of the crowd welled up around us. Darkness, wounds and all, lowered herself to one knee at the spot where the Dullahan's body had stood, her eyes closed as if in prayer.

Megumin called out to her hesitantly:

"Darkness, what are you doing?"

She answered without opening her eyes, as if talking to herself.

"…I'm praying. Dullahans are former knights, driven to undeath by

their rage when they are unjustly executed. I doubt he wanted to become a monster. I know we were enemies, but he deserves a prayer, at least…"

"I see…," murmured Megumin, but Darkness went on:

"There was Sedol, who spread ridiculous rumors that I was over-muscled under this armor, because he was angry that I'd beaten him at arm wrestling. Haines, who used to mock me on hot days: *Hey, Darkness, why don't you fan me with that huge sword of yours? Don't worry—I'm not afraid you'll hit me or anything!* Garil, who demanded to know why I would throw myself into a horde of monsters when I'd been in his party just one day. The Dullahan killed all of them. When I think about it, they were a bunch of good-for-nothings. But I…I can't quite bring myself to hate them."

"Um, I—I see," Megumin said. "T-tell you what. I'll listen to the whole story at the Guild Hall. Shall we go back?" Darkness didn't seem to hear Megumin's hurried attempt to change the subject. Eyes still closed, she murmured gently:

"I wish I could see them again… I wish we could share just one drink together…"

"W-wow …"

From behind her came a chorus of confused voices. Darkness started. Standing there were three embarrassed-looking men.

The three who Beldia had cut down.

Finally, one of them said apologetically:

"H-hey, I…I'm sorry. For a lot of stuff. We didn't know you felt… that way…"

"Y-yeah. I'm sorry, too. I shouldn'ta spread those rumors about you over a little arm-wrestling contest. Tell you what—next round's on me."

"I…I didn't know you were embarrassed about not being able to hit anything. I'm sorry, three."

Darkness was still kneeling in prayer, her eyes closed, but as the men apologized one after another, her cheeks grew redder and redder.

And here came Aqua to spoil the moment.

"How do you like that, Darkness? When you're as powerful as I am, a little death isn't enough to stop you! Aren't you happy? Now you can have a drink with your friends!"

I didn't suppose she had any sense she'd done anything wrong.

Darkness, however, realizing the men had heard everything she'd just said, sat down, covered her blushing face with both hands, and began to cry.

"Hey, hey," I said as brightly as I could. "This is great, right? C'mon, go get a drink!"

Darkness muttered through her hands:

"...Please kill me..."

"Aww, c'mon," I said. "You love it when people humiliate you! Hey, enjoy it—I could keep this up for days!"

Shoulders shaking, she groaned, "This is *not* the sort of humiliation I prefer!"

Epilogue

It was the day after we'd defeated Beldia.

I went to the Guild Hall alone, mulling over where we could go from here.

I was tasked with defeating the Demon King. But that meant Beldia was just the first in a parade of tough opponents I would have to face.

And if I did beat the Demon King—I could have one wish.

Or I could give up the whole thing and just try to live a quiet, comfortable life in this fantasy world.

…The answer was obvious.

I was a weak member of a weak class. I'd won that last battle literally by sheer Luck, and I couldn't rely on a plot contrivance like that again.

The thing to do was to live in peace, avoiding any danger.

I could use the knowledge I had from Japan to make something sellable.

I'd have a nice, safe job. Maybe do a simple quest now and then for some stimulation.

Those were the thoughts I was lost in as I arrived at the Guild Hall.

A nauseating smell hit me as I opened the door—a cloying mixture of sweat and alcohol.

Many of the town's adventurers had been at the bar since noon, celebrating their defeat of one of the Demon King's generals.

"Oh! Hey, Kazuma, you're late!" Aqua called cheerfully to me as I entered the hall. "The party's already started! Go get your money—pretty much everyone else here has already claimed their reward for beating the Dullahan. Myself included, of course! You can see how much of it they've drunk already, though."

I didn't understand why she seemed so pleased until she opened her purse and showed me how much she'd made as a reward. She just laughed and scratched her head, apparently having a genuinely good time.

Who had drunk their reward, exactly?

What was the drinking age in this world, anyway?

Most of the adventurers in the Guild Hall were so smashed they could barely walk.

I headed for the counter, skirting around the drunks.

Darkness and Megumin were already there.

"Oh, Kazuma, you're here. Go get your reward."

"We have been waiting for you, Kazuma. Listen! Darkness is being very mean to me. She says I am too young to drink."

"What do you m-mean?! That's not—!"

I left the two of them to banter, heading for the counter where the clerk stood.

I knew this clerk by now. When she saw me, for some reason, an unreadable expression came over her face.

"Ah, Mr.…Kazuma Satou, isn't it? We've been waiting for you."

They had?

Something about the way she spoke made me wary.

"Ahem… First, for you two…"

She handed one small bag to Darkness and another to Megumin.

Hey, where's my bag?

Before I could ask, the clerk said, "Um… Ahem. Actually, Mr. Kazuma, a special reward has been prepared for your party."

What's this?!

"Why just us?"

Practically before the question was out of my mouth, someone shouted: "'Cause you're the MVPs! Without you, we'd never have beaten that Dullahan!" A chorus of drunken agreement sounded around the room.

Wow... These guys...

I'd spent so long slaving away in this world, I hadn't realized how good it could be to you.

I was to accept the special reward on behalf of the four of us.

The clerk cleared her throat and began...

"Ahem! Kazuma Satou and his party, for their service above and beyond the call of duty in the defeat of the Demon King's general Beldia...are hereby awarded three hundred million eris!"

"Th-three—?" All four of us nearly choked.

The whole room had gone dead silent.

"Hey, Mr. Three-hundred-millionaire! How about a round?"

"Oh, Kazuma, my dear Kazuma! Won't you get me a little something to wet my whistle?"

One adventurer after another begged for a drink.

That reminded me...

"Hey, Darkness! Megumin! I'm thinking about scaling back our adventuring. With this windfall, I'd like to live the peaceful, *safe* life from here on out!"

"W-wait, but that means no more powerful enemies! What am I supposed to do? And whatever happened to defeating the Demon King?!"

"I, too, must object! I joined your party in order to defeat the Demon King and become known as the world's strongest spell-caster!"

The noise in the Guild Hall threatened to drown out their agitated voices.

The clerk handed me a slip of paper with an apologetic look.

It had an awful lot of zeroes on it.

Was the paper this world's equivalent of a check?

Aqua, in high spirits, tottered up next to me and glanced at the paper.

"Ahem, Mr. Kazuma—as it were, Ms. Aqua—the water you summoned washed away some of the buildings near the town gate and caused significant flood damage, and, well—you did succeed in defeating the Demon King's general, and no one would expect you to reimburse the full amount for damages, but they would like you to pay...at least a part..."

With that, the clerk turned away from us and retreated into a back room.

Megumin looked at the slip of paper in my hand and darted away.

I caught Aqua by the collar just as she was turning to flee, too.

All the other adventurers, guessing the size of the bill by the looks on our faces, made a show of minding their own business.

Darkness tapped her fingers on my shoulder as she did the math:

"A three-hundred-million-eris reward...less restitution of three hundred and forty million... Kazuma. I think for tomorrow's quest, we'd better find a very strong and very *profitable* enemy."

A wide smile crept over her face as she thought about it.

Was I going to have to spend the rest of my life in this insane world with these useless party members?

I closed my eyes, took a deep breath, and resolved to defeat the Demon King.

I had to get *out* of this good-for-nothing world!

FIN.

Afterword

First, thank you for picking up this book.

Second, nice to meet you! I'm Natsume Akatsuki.

Konosuba started life on a website called "I'm Gonna Be an Author!" and then Sneaker Bunko got in touch with me about turning it into a real book.

I can't even say how grateful I am.

Because that's how this book started, some of my readers probably already have an inkling where things are going from here.

That makes things difficult for me as a writer—I want to exceed my readers' expectations. So there's a good chance the story in the book will turn out differently from the one on the web. (I've already made several such changes in this volume.)

So if you think you know where things will go, watch out. You'll be reading along, and then one day, *bang!* Kazuma is heating some canned coffee over a fire when it explodes and kills him dead! Next volume, new main character. That's just the sort of crazy thing that could happen in the novel version. (Note: That is not actually going to happen.)

Let me say a few words about the story itself.

These are not the adventures of some kind, cool, butt-kicking hero.

Nor are they the tales of a boy who gains great power and then achieves his goal after trials and hardship.

No, the main character of this book is a guy who might help someone if he happens to notice them, depending on the circumstances and how he's feeling that day. A guy who doesn't always get it right, who wants a cute girlfriend, and who would give up doing anything productive if he came into a lot of money.

That's who we're dealing with here. Someone average. Human. A character trying to deal with the unjust realities of a harsh world even as he struggles along as the leader of a group of heroines, each of whom has a distinguishing personality trait.

He's nothing special—he's not the Chosen One or whatever. He doesn't have a great hidden power and so on. He's a little luckier than most people, is all.

Whether he fights or flees, he's learning about life one big, bad enemy at a time.

…Actually, I guess he doesn't learn much at all.

People don't change that easily, after all.

But I'm sure he'll prove his worth by the end of the story. Aren't you?

Back to the point of this afterword.

To all the editors, proofreaders, salespeople, and designers at Sneaker Bunko.

To Kurone Mishima for his wonderful illustrations, as well as my editor K, who had nothing but patience for an author who barely knew his right hand from his left.

This book exists because of your unflagging support and your refusal to give up on an exceptionally troublesome writer.

Thank you all so, so much.

I don't know what I can say to repay you for how wonderful you helped make this book, except that I'll work hard to make the next one even better.

Writing well may be the best way I can give back to you.

*   *   *

And finally…

To all those who read the book in its web form and offered their encouragement and support.

And above all, to those who picked this book when they needed something to read. You have my deepest gratitude.

Natsume Akatsuki

You were on the cover of Volume 1, Aqua... That means I am up next!

What are you talking about? Silly child. Pfft ha-ha-ha! I am a goddess and the undisputed heroine of this story! I'm going to be on *every* cover! We'll sell a hundred million copies in no time!

Aw, you are just a jealous old biddy!

A b-b-biddy?! Waaaah! Ohhh, Kazumaaa! Megumin's being *mean* to me!

...Hey, do the preview right.

Allow me. Volume 2 includes me getting beat up by a major enemy and Kazuma being cuckolded!

Did you just say "cuckolded"?

...No.

Guys, focus! Next volume!

I will appear in Volume 2!

?

WHO ARE YOU?!

As if you didn't know, Aqua!

?

...

KONOSUBA: GOD'S BLESSING ON THIS WONDERFUL WORLD 2

Love, Witches & Other Delusions!

COMING SOON!!

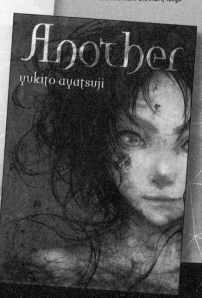